GW00857789

The Secret Trilogy

Books 1 – 3

Katrina Kahler

Copyright © KC Global Enterprises Pty Ltd

Table of Contents

Book 1

Mind Magic

The discovery...

When I decided to visit Sam that afternoon, there was no way that I expected to witness the scene in front of me. From my spot hidden amongst the clump of trees that bordered our properties, I had a fairly good view through the window of the upstairs room.

He had no idea I was watching.

It had been by chance that I looked up when I did. And that was when I caught him in action. The fear and confusion that gripped me right then were so intense that I stood frozen to the spot. It explained everything I'd seen happen at school and I knew instantly that he was to blame.

But how could he have fooled me for so long? And how many others knew his secret? That was the question on my lips as I stared in silent horror at what was unfolding right in front of me.

And then he glanced out the window.

It was as though he knew I was there. Watching. Silently watching. And I realized at last, that all the mysterious incidents and near disasters, suddenly made sense.

But the moment we made eye contact, I turned quickly and moved away.

I was afraid. I was suddenly frightened of the boy who I thought was my friend and I turned and raced home. Back to the sanctuary of my upstairs bedroom where I closed the door behind me and drew the curtains tightly shut.

At the same time, I knew he was there, through those bushes and on the other side, probably staring my way.

But what was I to do?

And who could I tell?

I had no idea.

And so I just sat down quietly on my bed, overwhelmed with despair.

How it all began...

I guess that moving to a new neighborhood is like stepping into the unknown. Not only is there a new house and a new bedroom to get used to, but there are even more important things to worry about, like a new school and new friends. For a twelve-year-old girl, that is definitely what matters most! Those important details were foremost in my mind when we turned the corner into the street leading to our new home.

But when I noticed the run-down ramshackle place next door, my previous concerns were momentarily forgotten.

Although our property was separated from the adjoining one by a line of dense bush, I managed to get a good look at the house next to ours as we drove slowly past. My first impression was that it might be abandoned because it was definitely in a state of disrepair. But my mom confirmed that there were actually people living there and that one of them happened to be a boy my age.

That news sparked my interest immediately. And I wondered about the people who lived in the old house that looked like it might fall down around them.

Glancing towards it, I felt an unexpected tingle work its way down my spine. It was an odd sensation that caused goose bumps to appear on my skin, even though it was a warm day and the sun was shining brightly.

For some strange reason, I got the distinct impression we were being watched.

Then just as we pulled into our driveway, I glimpsed a slight movement behind the curtain at the front window and felt certain that someone was peering out.

My dad parked our car in front of a pair of green double garage doors and when I hopped out, I tried to look through the bush to the other side. From where I stood, however, my view was blocked by the thick foliage that grew in that very spot.

What surprised me though was when Jasper, our three-year-old long-haired terrier jumped off the back seat of the car where he'd been sitting beside me and stood stock still and alert, staring intensely towards the shrubbery. And then, within seconds, he began to bark. It was as though he could sense that something was amiss, that something on the other side of the closely cropped trees required investigation.

But that would have to wait, I decided quickly, as I tugged on his collar and led him along the pavement towards our front door. The last thing I wanted was for my excited dog to go racing into the neighbor's yard and begin yelping loudly to get their attention. That was not the way I wanted to meet our new neighbors.

So I had to curb my own curiosity, at least until later in the afternoon, and make an effort to help my parents unpack some of the many boxes that were already being unloaded and carried inside. The removal van had pulled up right behind our car and the driveway was a hive of activity.

At the sudden sound of rolling thunder right above us, I looked up and saw that dark clouds had quickly amassed in the sky overhead. Although where the brewing storm had come from, I had no idea, as the weather had seemed so warm and clear only moments earlier. So with one last sideways glance back towards the row of shrubs, I made my way inside the house with Jasper in tow beside me.

Taking the stairs two at a time, I headed directly to the upper level where my bedroom was waiting to be chosen. And with a rising excitement at the thought of exploring the large home and the garden beyond, I put images of the dilapidated house next to ours out of my mind, as I went in search of a suitable room to call my own.

It had been a kind of peace offering by my mom giving me the choice of whatever room on the upper floor I wanted. At the time she'd said it, it hadn't meant very much as I was too upset about leaving our old house and my school and all my friends behind.

But now that we'd arrived, I somehow sensed there was excitement to be found in this new place and that things would unfold in a way I had never expected. And so with eager anticipation, I made my way along the walkway leading past various rooms, Jasper panting at my side with each step I took.

When I opened the heavy oak door at the end of the hallway, I knew instantly that I needed to look no further. The room seemed to beckon me into its welcoming interior and as I stepped through the doorway, I glanced curiously around. That was when I noticed the amazingly large oval-shaped window on the far wall and when I approached it to look outside, I caught glimpses of the house next door.

Once again, I stopped for a moment and wondered about the boy who lived there. I had no idea, however, how my life would become intertwined with his, or the secret that would eventually become exposed to me.

Right then, there was no way whatsoever that I could possibly have imagined what life had in store. And I'm quite sure that if anyone had ever tried to warn me, I would never have believed them.

Sam....

My real name is Sam but I'm known as Mind Freak. In the virtual world anyway.

The kids who I connect with online have no idea of my real power, the mind magic that gives me a superhuman strength they can only dream of. This power, the one that I possess, makes me capable of crazy, supernatural and even paranormal activity.

Sounds intense, right?

Well, it really is! And much more so than you could possibly imagine. Unless you see me in action, that is.

But I'm sworn to secrecy. I can't let anyone know. They all think I'm weird enough already. I certainly don't need to make things worse for myself.

And then I met Tess, my new neighbor. Well, I didn't actually meet her straight away, but I certainly *saw* her. And that's when everything changed.

It was Sunday afternoon and I was in my room playing computer games, which was absolutely normal for me. I had little else to do on weekends and without my computer games, I have no idea what I would have done to pass the time.

But that afternoon, right at the crucial moment when I really needed to concentrate or I'd be shot down dead by my online enemy, I heard what sounded like a dog barking just outside my open window. I tried to switch off from the sound, but the yapping was too distracting and I struggled to give the game the attention it needed.

Just as the loud ruckus became even more intense, the enemy came after my entire team and within seconds, the game was over. And I knew that my team would blame me. It was my fault that we'd all been shot down.

Frustrated and annoyed, I took off the headset and looked at my shaking hands. I was usually able to lead my team to victory. It made me feel good to be in control and that was very different from the world I really lived in. But that afternoon, I did not get the result I wanted.

Alongside me, I heard the drip of raindrops hitting the metal pot that sat on the floor. Earlier that day the sky had been completely clear, and then an unexpected storm had passed over. But finally, it had slowed to a few irregular drops.

It was almost seven o'clock in the evening, the sun was going down, and I could still hear that dog. I knew we had new neighbors, but I had done nothing to welcome them. My mother had probably already called into their house to say hello and introduce herself. And knowing my mom, she would have been sure to take a plate of organic cookies along with her pack of tarot cards that she used to tell people their future. She never went anywhere without those.

She was obsessed with the supernatural and actually made a living out of doing psychic readings for people who wanted to know what their future held. People came from near and far to learn what was in store, and she had gained quite a reputation.

The fact that a lot of people thought she was weird and strange, didn't deter her in the slightest. On the other hand, I, myself, thought what she did was pretty cool. Although I'd never admit that to any of my classmates.

The barking noise continued and I pulled aside the sheer white curtain that covered my window so I could get a better view. The dog was on our side of the property and it appeared to have been attracted by something hiding in the bushes below; probably a small animal of some type that was trying desperately to escape the yapping dog that was intent on finding it.

The owner of the dog, who was dressed in a green raincoat, was trying to encourage it to go back home, but the dog was reluctant to move. I could not tell the identity of the person at first, but then I caught sight of wispy blond hair and immediately, I was drawn closer to the window. I don't know why I felt compelled to stand there and stare like some kind of weird stalker, but I seemed to be frozen to the spot, unable to take my eyes from the figure in front of me.

Realizing that she was being watched, she looked up towards the window, where I was trying to remain hidden from view. The hood that had covered her head from the rain, fell away and her long blond hair was abruptly revealed. I decided right then and there that she was perfect. And when we made eye contact, she seemed to see through to my very soul.

When she waved to me, I suddenly found myself doing the same. My mouth was agape at seeing a girl who looked like her in my very own backyard. And the fact that she was trying to get my attention, had caught me by complete surprise.

Then I saw her smile and instantly it lit up the dark dreary existence of my life like a series of fireworks shooting into the blackness of the night. I tried to say something, but my mouth was dry and there was no way that I wanted to attract more attention to myself.

"Hi, I'm Tess," she called from her spot below. "I just moved in next door with my parents. This is my dog, Jasper."

She was expecting me to reply but I just couldn't do it. The tough soldier of the virtual world, who had just been willing to lead his team into battle had been replaced by the shy awkward boy that everybody knew me to be; in real life anyway. I was a loner. The kids at school looked at what my mother did for a living and made me out to be some kind of weird loser as well.

With a last glance at the unexpected vision beneath my window, I moved quickly out of sight. I felt so stupid for not saying anything but I could not bring myself to respond. That probably wasn't the best first impression but being awkward was a trait I'd developed and that particular occasion was no different to any other.

I knew straight away that I'd probably have to add her to the list of people who thought of me as a loser. The problem was that I really didn't know how to talk to girls. Ever since my father had deserted us, I'd only had my mom for company and that certainly hadn't helped me to be confident around other kids, girls especially.

Abruptly, my little self-pity session was interrupted by the sound of my mother's voice calling from the bottom of the stairs. "Sam, our new neighbor is at the door. Can you come down to meet her?"

I couldn't believe that this was happening. I didn't want to meet the pretty girl who had appeared in my backyard. Well, I did want to meet her but not right then. It was awkward and embarrassing and I did not want this first meeting to be because my mother had forced me to come to the front door.

"Sam?" she called again, waiting impatiently for a response.

She was the one who had taught me how to have manners and show respect to my elders and all that other stuff that parents insist on teaching their kids, but that had not helped my confidence issues. And there was no way I wanted to be embarrassed by my mother right then.

"I'm getting ready to do my homework. I have that big test in the morning and I really don't have time."

I knew she wouldn't try to force the issue. She was not much for arguments. And she always tried to avoid making me angry. She was well aware of what could happen if she did.

But when there was no reply, I guessed that she'd given up on the idea and I breathed a sigh of relief. I had just avoided embarrassment for one day, but then I wondered if I would see the girl the following day at school. There were a couple of private schools in the area, but mine was the main public one and could possibly be the one that she'd chosen to go to.

If that were the case, I could only hope that she hadn't managed to get a good look at me when she saw me through the window. I just wanted to stay incognito and invisible. It was much easier that way. As much as I really did want to meet her, I preferred to avoid attracting attention. It was hard enough surviving at school, especially with Jake Collins around. But then that was another story altogether. And I tried to stay out of his way as much as possible.

Being smaller than the rest of the kids in my class made me a prime target for Jake and when no one else was around to pick on, he would zoom in on me. It was bad enough that we had to survive on my mother's small income from psychic readings, but I also had to deal with the stuff that went on at school.

Although so far, he'd only pushed me around a little and shoved me into my locker a couple of times which was nothing compared to what he'd done to others. I didn't need that kind of abuse and I wasn't sure what I would do if he ever became too physical. Sometimes I was afraid of myself and I had every reason to feel that way.

I thought back to the last time I had seen my dad. He went out to buy some bread and never came back. Ever since I've wanted to track him down and shake the truth out of him.

Why did he leave without saying a word? How could he just leave my mom and I alone like that? I wanted to remind him that he'd left us to fend for ourselves and that our lives had been a struggle ever since. And most importantly, maybe he had an explanation for the strange phenomena I'd found myself capable of. That was definitely something I wanted answers to.

Eventually, I did get my school work done but that was after checking the status of my computer game and the messages that had appeared on my board. The members of my team who had survived the attack were praising my skill and the way I'd managed to save most of our men. I had no idea who some of the players were in real life, but they were my friends from the hours of six-thirty till eight-thirty in the evening. They were the hours I was given permission by my mom to have access to the one thing that helped to keep me sane.

During those times I would change my identity and take on a whole new personality. Rather than being my usual real-life self, the loser that everyone seemed to think I was, I'd become a tough soldier who was willing to do practically anything to get the job done. It even had me thinking that I should join the army when I was old enough to leave school.

At least I'd find some discipline and become part of a real-life team rather than just a virtual one. I didn't want to think about how hard the army would be, but instead, hoped it would be worth it in the end.

Later that night, after working my way through a heap of homework that my teacher had insisted was overdue, I went to bed with a list of numbers and mathematical equations spinning in my head. I thought that I had a pretty good understanding of all the work we'd covered during the semester and was probably ready for the test. I just hoped I wouldn't freeze up at the critical moment. I hated exams, they made me nervous, and I could hardly wait to get this one over with.

The thought of the test I'd be forced to sit through the following morning, along with the image of the girl next door were what played on my mind as I tossed and turned trying to sleep.

Tess, she had said her name was.

I repeated the name in my head, liking the sound of it.

That and the picture of her long blond hair and perfect features were what kept me awake for the next hour or so. But finally, my tiredness got the best of me and eventually, I fell asleep.

Numbers, equations and the face of a very pretty new neighbor filling my dreams.

Unfair...

I had on a pair of jeans and a white shirt with a black stripe down each side. I was wearing old tattered white no-name sneakers and a jacket that was a hand me down from one of my mother's clients. It had become faded and old looking but it was still my favorite. At least it was a lot better than the other things that I'd been given to choose from. But there was nothing I could do about the clothes in my cupboard. There was little enough money as it was and definitely none spare to pay for the 'cool' clothes and shoes that a lot of the other kids wore.

"Sam... Sam... Sam."

I heard my name being called, but it seemed almost foreign. Nobody ever went out of their way to approach me by name. I usually hung out on my own and most of the time, the other kids chose to avoid me.

"You are Sam, aren't you?"

I looked up from where I was sitting by a large tree, waiting for the bell to signal the start of classes, and there she was, staring in my direction.

"Do I know you?" I was trying to pretend I had no idea who she was, but in reality, I had recognized her immediately.

"I'm your new neighbor. I saw you looking out your window and then I met your mom. She seemed really nice."

The friendly smile on her face was not one I had expected. Rather than being friendly in return, I felt my face flush a bright red and I felt more awkward than ever.

"Oh, hey," I stammered in response, not sure what else to say.

But then the bell sounded, and we were surrounded by kids heading to class. Grateful for the distraction, I turned around and followed them, the overwhelming embarrassment taking a firm hold in my gut.

I was sure I'd just made a complete fool of myself. But she'd caught me off-guard and I didn't know what to say or do. I definitely wasn't used to girls like her talking to me. Most of the time, I was like an invisible ghost that they chose to ignore. And to have her up close like that, actually interested in meeting me, was not something I was used to.

Aware of the red flush covering my face, I kept my head down and made my way into class, taking my seat over by the window. I sat next to a nerdy girl called Jasmine. But that was fine because she didn't seem bothered to have me sitting beside her. Her main focus was to concentrate on every word the teacher said. Getting straight A's on her report card was all that mattered.

It actually came in handy that she was so smart because if I didn't know the answer to a question, I just had to look at her work and there it was.

Unfortunately, that morning our teacher had separated our desks and I wasn't able to copy. I just had to hope that I'd done enough revision the night before and would be able to answer most of the questions on my own.

Just as we were about to start, I glanced up to see my new neighbor, Tess, walking through the open doorway. She'd obviously been placed in my class and I stared in fascination at the pretty girl who had just entered the room. Her long blond hair hung around her shoulders and she brushed away the stray wisps that fell across her eyes. When our teacher introduced her and she scanned the faces who were all looking towards her, the expression on each as curious as my own, I watched as her eyes fell on mine, lighting up in recognition.

Feeling the red flush creep over my face once again, I looked down at my desk, desperate to avoid any eye contact with the new girl that every kid in the class was intently focusing on right then. It was obviously tough being a new kid and she was probably pleased to see a familiar face but I was the last person she should be acknowledging. I knew that, everyone else knew that, but she was yet to learn that simple fact.

Once again, I did not want to draw any attention to myself. I'd learned on several occasions it was better to stay under the radar. So I breathed a sigh of relief when I realized she'd been assigned a spare desk at the back, alongside a couple of girls. Keeping my head down, I pretended to concentrate on the test paper that had been placed in front of me.

While waiting to be given permission to start, a fleeting thought crossed my mind. What a way to begin your first day at a new school! To be faced with a math test the minute you walked in the classroom door…would be the worst thing ever!

Welcome to my world, Tess. Yes, life did suck sometimes and I guess that morning was one of those times. At least I wasn't the only one who'd be feeling a bit overwhelmed right then. But in reality, apart from Jasmine and a few other super smart kids in our class, there were probably a lot of others in the room who were feeling at least a little overwhelmed as well.

And when I glanced at Jake who sat nearby, I could clearly see the anxious look on his face and was well aware that he would definitely struggle with the test in front of him.

At least I was able to get some satisfaction out of that small detail. He may be a kid that others looked up to but schoolwork was definitely one thing he was not good at.

Yeah, Jake. Sometimes life just isn't fair!

Unable to resist, I took a quick peek towards the back of the room and saw the same anxious look on Tess's face. But instead of smirking, this time all I felt was sympathy. Surely our teacher could have given her something else to do.

Sighing with resignation, I turned the test over and began to work, trying the entire time to focus on the equations in front of me instead of all the other things that kept creeping into my head.

Embarrassment…

As if having to do a Math exam first thing on a Monday morning wasn't bad enough, it seemed that my day was destined to become progressively worse.

The next unwelcome event happened in the middle of our lunch break. I'd just left the dining hall and was heading outside to sit in my favorite spot.

This was situated under a shady tree which had massive overhanging branches creating a small secluded area to sit in. It was a fairly isolated location and I could sit there and not be bothered by anyone, especially Jake Collins, whom I always tried to avoid.

In my hand was a book that I was really keen to check out. Just before lunch, our class had visited the library for our weekly borrowing session, which was scheduled at the same time every Monday.

During that time, the library teacher always tried to encourage kids to borrow books and she repeated the same phrase every week.

"Reading is the most important skill of all! The more you read, the better a reader you'll become and the more knowledge you'll learn."

Heaps of kids constantly had overdue books, so they managed to avoid having to borrow. But this weekly library session was something I'd begun to look forward to.

The main reason was that our school had a really cool section on outer space and this, along with pretty much any science fiction topic was something I could not get enough of. I was almost as obsessed with these things as I was with my computer games.

As it turned out, I'd realized that if I searched hard enough, I'd find some great books hidden away on the library shelves. The week before I'd discovered a book that I could not put down. It was so good that I read it in one night. All about a guy who had turned his power to evil because of the way that he was treated by others, it was a story that I could easily relate to. It was almost a detailed description of what my future life could become…if I wasn't careful that was.

My latest find was a really interesting book about some outer galaxies that had been discovered. Apparently, in the last ten years, the number of known satellite galaxies had doubled and I was keen to find out what I could. That was the best thing when it came to astronomy, it was all so mysterious and scientists still had so much to learn.

Ever since I was a little kid, I'd been interested in anything to do with outer space. At one stage I even had a make-believe friend that I told my mom was an alien. That little creature was something that had appeared in my imaginary world just after my dad left. I guess my imaginary friend was what I needed at the time but whatever the reason, I totally believed that he existed.

As far as aliens are concerned, I still believe they do exist and the book I had in my hand had an entire section devoted to alien life on other planets. I could hardly wait to read it but as it turned out, I did not get the chance; not during that lunch break, anyway.

I had my eyes glued to the pages of the open book and was not watching where I was going. Of course, as luck would have it, I walked right into Jake Collins who happened to be standing in the middle of the pavement in front of me. And I guess it was an invitation he found impossible to resist.

"Hey, loser. Watch where you're going!" His loud voice carried across the area and instantly, I felt several pairs of eyes looking in our direction, his entire group of friends included.

With an audience looking on and ready and waiting for some action, he took the opportunity to draw as much attention as possible. Shoving me roughly out of his way, I fell back and overbalanced onto the pavement behind me.

This caused the book I was holding to fall from my grasp onto the ground. Turning a bright shade of red for the second time that day, I got to my feet while at the same time reaching for the fallen book. But it was abruptly kicked out of my reach.

"You are such a klutz, freak. Maybe you should have known that was going to happen. Don't you have psychic powers like your mom?" Jake laughed loudly and his crew of followers joined in, the scene in front of them an instant source of entertainment.

Ignoring them all, I reached for the book, but Jake continued to kick it away from my grip. He was finding the situation funnier than ever and his loud laughter rang in my ears. All I wanted was to grab the book and get away from him, but he was making that impossible. He even stooped so low that he stepped on my fingers a couple of times in the process.

The sound of his raucous laughter filled me with shame and I could feel my anger mounting. Just as the throbbing heat inside my head felt ready to explode, I caught sight of a passing teacher who realized what Jake was up to.

"Jake Collins, what do you think you're doing?" Miss Hodgkins, who was one of the grade seven teachers, glared sternly towards him.

"Nothing, Miss," Jake responded quickly as he raised his hands in mock surrender.

"Do I have to send you to the principal, yet again?" Her frown of disapproval and strict tone stopped him in his tracks but still, he could not resist a satisfied smirk.

"We were just playing around. Sam knows that don't you, Sam?"

She glanced at me and all I could do was stare back, shamefaced and humiliated, the burning sensation in my head continuing to throb. But when a different problem suddenly broke out amongst a group of kids behind her, she was forced to move quickly away in order to deal with it. All she had time for was a word of warning, reminding Jake to behave himself.

As he walked away, a smug grin stuck to his face, he had one parting kick at the book still remaining on the ground. In true Jake style, his aim was perfect and the book landed smack bang in the middle of a nearby puddle of water.

All I could do was bend down and pick up the soaking wet book and shake it out in the hope of draining the water off. I just prayed that it would survive, otherwise, I knew I'd be made to pay for the cost of replacing it.

Not daring to look back at Jake, I headed towards my lone spot under the tree. With each step, I tried to control the throbbing in my head. It was a power desperate to escape and give him what he deserved. Tempted to let him have it, I had to fight the impulse, knowing full well that if I didn't, I'd be the one facing the principal instead of him.

Being a little older than the rest of us had made him bigger and stronger than everyone else in our year level. He also had the power to intimidate. It was something he thrived on and he was often looking for a new target. For me, the reason for this was obvious, although knowing this hadn't helped me in the slightest. Most kids already thought I was weird and I was a prime candidate for his bullying. I was also yet to do anything about it.

Deep down, I knew he used the bullying to make him feel better about himself. He was hopeless with school work and always got low grades so he tried to make up for that in other ways. Being physically bigger than everyone else, he was able to use that to his advantage.

One thing he was good at though, was sport. His skill, not just on the football field but in pretty much every athletic area, was far better than anyone else's and because of this, all the other kids held him in awe. But to me, he was a jerk and I just tried to stay out of his way.

Humiliated, I continued along the pavement towards my loner spot under the tree. And then I noticed a group of girls watching me. They'd obviously just witnessed the whole incident with Jake, which added to my shame. The worst part was that the new girl, Tess, was standing amongst them, and was also one of the ones staring openly.

Adding further to my embarrassment, I caught sight of Samantha Evans, one of the girls in our grade and also a part of the cool group, leading Tess away. When she started whispering in Tess's ear and glancing back towards me, I knew for sure that she was telling Tess to stay away from the "loser" kid with the weird psychic lady for a mother.

I could see that already; Tess had managed to attract the attention of the cool crowd. She'd only just arrived and they were encouraging her to join their group. To fit in so easily was something I could only imagine. And I looked on in envy as Tess's new friends chatted and laughed amongst themselves.

I'd lived in our town all my life and the only attention I was given consisted of strange looks and sniggering remarks, claiming my house was haunted. Most of them didn't want to venture any further than my front gate. Although, there were some who decided they needed to ring the doorbell, just for the fun of it. Then of course, when my mom answered the door there was never anyone there.

Now I had a new neighbor who had actually tried to talk to me. But I'd obviously wrecked any chance of that happening. After what she'd just witnessed, there was no way she'd ever want to hang out with me, especially since Samantha had got in her ear.

Accepting my loser status for what it was, I made my way towards the tree; the dripping wet book hanging from my fingertips.

Sitting down on the grass, alone as usual, I turned the pages of the book in my hands, taking extra care not to tear the wet edges.

Escape...

Something happened on the bus ride home that I had not been expecting. I boarded the bus as usual, and as usual, I headed down the aisle to about half way and sat next to the window, dumping my backpack on the seat beside me.

I always chose the same location, never too close to the back as that was where the cool kids sat; and never too close to the front either, as that was claimed by all the nerds of the school. I did not belong with them and I definitely did not belong with the kids at the back either. I was pretty much in a category all of my own, so I always chose the middle.

But just as the bus was pulling away from the curb, I heard the sound of a voice beside me. At first, I ignored it, thinking that the girl must obviously be speaking to someone else. But when the question was repeated, I turned in her direction.

"Can I sit here?"

Feeling my face turn a dark shade of red, I raised my eyebrows and managed to speak. "Here?"

Surely, I'd been mistaken and had not heard her correctly. When I took a quick glance around and saw that there were plenty of other available seats on the bus, it confirmed my suspicions. I had definitely been mistaken.

But she nodded her head, indicating that yes, she actually

was referring to the seat alongside mine and that she did want to sit there. Quickly grabbing my bag, I shoved it onto the floor at my feet and moved over to make some room.

Edging closer to the window, I glanced out of the corner of my eye at the girl alongside me, not daring to make eye contact. But when she began talking, I was forced to look at her.

"I see you're into astronomy?" she asked curiously.

It was more of a question than a statement, and I raised my eyebrows in surprise.

"A...astronomy?" I stammered my reply, wondering why she would be asking and how she could possibly know about my fascination with anything related to outer space.

"I noticed the book you borrowed from the library today. So I guessed it must be something you're interested in."

Her explanation caught me by surprise. First of all, I was trying to come to terms with the fact that Tess was actually sitting next to me. But the realization that she'd taken notice of what I had borrowed from the library that day really put me off guard.

Without waiting for a reply, she continued, "I'm addicted to all that stuff. It's so amazing, don't you think? The fact that there are entire galaxies out there that we don't even know about. It's incredible!"

Dumbfounded, all I could do was nod my head. I was lost for words and wasn't sure how to respond. I'd already embarrassed myself enough for one day and was worried that whatever I said would sound lame, so I preferred to just nod in agreement instead.

Then I heard the voices of the kids in the seat behind us. And I was sure that Tess must have heard them too.

"What's she sitting next to him for?"

"She's new. She'll soon figure out how weird he is."

The sniggering continued but all I could do was sit in awkward silence and stare down at my lap. Until I felt a sudden urge to speak.

Without hesitating for another moment, I turned towards Tess and the words poured out. Although I didn't really want her to move, I felt obligated to warn her.

"It's cool if you want to sit someplace else. Things could get tough for you if you hang out with me. You're really better off sitting somewhere else."

She nodded her head, "Do you really think I'm going to listen to them?"

After a couple of minutes, the bus pulled to stop outside our houses. Grateful that I had the chance to escape from the teasing from the fools at the back of the bus, I stood and waited impatiently for her to move into the aisle. I just wanted to get off the bus and disappear.

The thick screen of bush that bordered the perimeter of my property could be seen from the bus window. Beyond that bush was the inner sanctuary of my bedroom and it was calling me. It was my safe zone and I could not get there quickly enough. Without another word, we made our way down the aisle towards the exit and stepped onto the pavement, ignoring her feeble attempt to say goodbye, I put my head down and rushed to my house.

Her words, "See you at school tomorrow," faded into oblivion behind me as I cut through the bush and found the track that would lead me to the place I needed to be right then.

And with each step I took, I could feel her piercing gaze boring into my back as she stood staring after me.

Loser...

Dropping my school bag on the floor of my room, I slumped into the chair in front of my computer and switched it on, ignoring my mom's warning voice in my head.

"Computer games from Monday to Friday are only allowed between the hours of six-thirty and eight-thirty at night," she exclaimed on a regular basis. "School work comes first!"

She was always threatening to ban my computer time completely if I didn't follow the rules, but she was fighting a losing battle with that one. Hidden away in my attic style bedroom, she had little idea of what I was up to. And she was rarely at home in the afternoons anyway. Not that it would've made any difference as I was determined to play regardless. Once school was over, I had the virtual world to look forward to. Apart from homework, there was little else to do. And at least when I was gaming, I wasn't treated like some useless loser.

Online, I was a hero. The other kids had no idea of my real identity of course, which was what made the games so much fun. I could be another person entirely and with all my gaming skills, no one ever had a bad word to say. My squad usually had the biggest survival rate. And most of the time it was because I'd been elected the leader of the mission.

Everyone had made up gaming names. Crazy Dude, Phantom, and War Fiend were just a few. But my name,

Mind Freak was known by everyone. I constantly had requests to join my squad. But I was very selective. I knew that some of them were from my school. I recognized their voices and the way they spoke and there was no way I was going to have them on my team.

It was my chance for revenge, even if it was only via a computer screen. The highlights of my day were the moments when I shot them down, or when my squadron managed to blast their players. I just wished that Jake was a part of it all, I could definitely have some fun playing against him. Unfortunately, I'd heard that computer games were not really his thing. He was probably too dumb anyway.

Keeping my identity secret was the biggest thrill. There was no way anyone would suspect that the loner kid at school could possibly be leading their squad on the battlefield. It was a bit of a joke really. The fact that I was actually in charge of the games they were all obsessing over and were totally addicted to was completely ironic. If only they knew!

Sometimes I imagined telling them, letting them in on my true online gaming identity. They wouldn't think me such a loser then. But I preferred to keep that fact a secret. It gave me a quiet satisfaction to know what I was capable of. And I just filed that piece of information away, along with my other deep dark secret that I didn't dare to tell anyone.

That afternoon, the idea of Minecraft or any of my other favorite games did not interest me at all. I was not in the frame of mind for gaming and I stared at the blank computer screen in frustration.

The events of the day played in my head. Almost as if on rewind, the scenes repeated themselves over and over and I could not remove the look on Tess's face as she witnessed the incident with Jake during lunch break. But to top that off with what had happened on the bus, just made it so much worse.

If I thought there could ever be a chance to hang out with a girl like her, then I was wrong.

Such an idiot.

No. Not an idiot. A total loser!

And throwing myself on my bed, I squeezed my eyes shut, trying desperately to stop the flow of tears that threatened at the corners of my eyes.

To cry like a baby… that was really heading into Loser Ville.

But then, maybe that's where I really belonged.

The cool crowd...

When I walked into school the next morning, I kept my head down. Although I made certain to stay aware of who or what was in my path. One thing I was grateful for was that Tess had not been on the bus, as I was dreading having to face her again.

I just wished that I could go back and start over. Repeat every embarrassing event from the time she had appeared beneath my bedroom window to the moment she sat next to me on the bus the next afternoon. Experience it all again and change everything.

I would have introduced myself when I spotted her in the garden chasing her dog, maybe even offered to help. I would have watched where I was going when I headed down the pavement with the book in my hand. And I would have made sure I was ready and willing to talk to her on the bus...rather than sitting alongside her and staring like an idiot.

"Yeah, I love science fiction. And anything to do with outer space is so cool. If you want to have a look at the book I borrowed, that's fine. Just let me know."

I pictured the scene in my head. The words I could have said and the way I would have liked it to play out, repeated on rewind over and over in my mind. And instead of the usual sick sensation, I felt a warm fuzziness starting to grow in the pit of my belly. Until I spotted Jake that was. And instantly, all my daydreams melted quickly away.

He was in the midst of a group of kids, all his followers and all the prettiest girls in our class surrounding him. But right in the thick of it all was Tess, the smile on her face beaming widely.

She was clearly the center of their attention and it looked like every cool kid in our grade was desperate to talk to her.

Realizing that she must've caught the early bus or had perhaps been given a ride to school, I felt the warm fuzzy sensation revert quickly to the sinking feeling that I'd become so accustomed to.

Heading towards my spot under the tree, I kept my head down and my thoughts to myself.

All I could do was wait for the bell to ring for class so I could get the day over with.

It was just another boring morning at school with little to look forward to.

Nothing had changed.

But if that was the case, then why did I feel so sad?

Unexpected...

The day passed by in a bit of a blur. I managed to avoid Jake, whose concentration was obviously on the new girl. At least it was giving me and all the other kids who suffered from his stupid remarks, a break from his bullying. I also avoided Tess, although that wasn't hard as she was smothered with so much attention that she had more than likely forgotten I even existed.

That was what I believed right then. I decided that I should forget all about the pretty girl who had moved into the house next to mine, however, I soon discovered that things were not as they seemed.

It all came about in the dining hall. Everyone had filed in and were lining up with their trays ready to collect the lunch on offer. That day's choices were amongst my favorites and I grabbed an oversized beef burger, a plate of fries and a soda. Then, in a split second decision, with my mom's insistent voice ringing in my head, I decided to take an apple as well.

"Make sure you eat some fruit during the day," she had reminded me just that morning.

Surely the large bowl of mixed fruit that she'd prepared for my breakfast, was enough for one day's intake but I felt obliged to do as she'd asked. Being able to access the dining hall for lunch was a huge treat and it didn't happen often. She usually gave me a packed lunch to take to school that was full of healthy home-baked food. For one thing, she didn't like me eating too much junk and as well as that, the cost of a dining hall lunch wasn't cheap. But she'd had an increase in business lately and said that she could afford it, for that day at least.

Trying to remain inconspicuous, I headed towards a table near the back that nobody was using, all the while looking forward to the delicious burger on my plate. And when I sat down, I dived in with a huge bite. My mom was a vegetarian and never cooked meat. So I was enjoying every bit of the burger in my hands. It was definitely a tasty change from the lentil burgers that she made for me at home.

Focused on my food, I was oblivious to what was going on around me and I did not see Tess approach. In fact, I was completely unaware of her presence until she sat down beside me.

It seemed that she had a habit of sneaking up on people. Well, it was the second time it had happened to me and I wondered later if it was something she made a habit of doing. This time though, she didn't ask for permission to join me, she just slid along the bench next to me and put her tray of food down alongside mine.

"Hey!"

It was a one-word greeting and I looked towards her, startled. My mouth was full of burger, and once again I found myself unable to speak. Trying to chew and swallow at the same time was not a good look and I attempted to gulp down the mouthful of food, realizing that all of a sudden, my appetite had vanished.

I smiled, despite the fact that I felt a little out of place. She deserved so much better than what I had to offer. Why she was even showing any interest was a mystery that was known only to her. Then I wondered for a moment if she felt sorry for me. Was that the reason she was even bothering at all?

If that's what it was though, I decided abruptly that I wasn't interested. I did not want to be a charity case and I hated the thought of her pitying me. I'd rather just stick to myself and my loner status. But her next words caught me by surprise and I realized that I may have misjudged her after all.

"I have this really cool telescope. It was a present for my twelfth birthday and last night I set it up in my room. You should come over some time and take a look."

I stared at her in disbelief and as usual, found myself lost for words. She actually wanted to hang out with me. It was such a strange concept that I was struggling to believe she was being genuine. So much so, that a mixture of confused thoughts raced through my head.

Had Jake put her up to this? Or had her new friends dared her to do it?

Quickly scanning the dining hall, I half expected to see kids looking in my direction, laughing hysterically. But no one appeared to have even noticed us.

 "Do you want to come over tonight?" she continued, in her friendly up-front manner. "That's if you're not busy? My telescope is super high-powered so it works really well."

I could not help the smile that was creeping onto my face. It was obvious by her tone and her manner that she was not joking around, she really did mean what she was saying.

"Um, yeah," I replied, trying desperately not to be too awkward. "That sounds cool. I'm not busy, so yeah, I'll come over."

She smiled in return, clearly pleased with my response. And without bothering to say anything else, she started munching on the food in front of her.

Following her lead, I returned to my burger and as I took another bite, my mind reeled with excitement. It was such an unfamiliar sensation that I considered pinching myself to be sure I wasn't dreaming.

The prettiest girl in the grade, the new girl that everyone was trying to be friends with, had approached me. And asked me to hang out. Even after witnessing my embarrassing incident the day before, and being told by her friends what they thought of me. Regardless of all that, she was still happy to sit with me in the dining hall, in full view of everyone. It seemed too good to be true.

But then I saw Jake looking in my direction, and my excitement quickly turned to one of dread. The expression on his face told me everything. His usual smirk had been transformed into a deep scowl. He was not at all impressed. I really did not have to be a mind reader to work that one out. And when he stood and began to make his way to our table, I felt my skin crawl with anticipation of what would happen next.

With his hands slung deep in his pockets, he sauntered over, the confident smirk returning to his face. Then, sliding along the seat next to Tess, he made sure she was sandwiched tightly between the two of us.

"I know that you're new here, Tess. So I'm doing you a favor by telling you this." He stared intensely at her, not a shy bone in his body.

For a moment, I envied his confidence. People appeared to instantly sit up and take notice of every word he said. Girls in particular. They seemed to go crazy around him. How did he do that? How did he have that effect? It was weird. And I couldn't understand it. But there was one thing that I did understand very clearly. I was jealous.

"You really need to know before it's too late," he continued, that deep confident voice of his holding her attention. "Sam is a loser that wears old hand-me-down clothes. He gets them from the Salvation Army. His mother is a witch and you really shouldn't be seen talking to kids like him."

The familiar anger sat deep in my stomach and I held my hands beneath the table out of sight. My fingers were gripping the chair and I could feel my fingernails scratching the surface. I wanted to ignore his comments, block him out completely, but I was struggling to control myself.

The smug look on his face clearly showed that he expected her to take in every word. That's what everyone else did and I was fairly certain that he thought that this occasion would be no different. As it turned out though, the new girl was not like all the rest.

"I think I can pick my own friends." Tess's tone was not at all pleased and I'm not sure who was more shocked by her response, Jake or myself.

Inside my head, I murmured a silent cheer, encouraging her on. No one ever spoke to Jake like that. And from the corner of my eye, I tried to gauge what he would do next.

But then, as if having second thoughts, Tess continued. "Sam lives right next door to me. And I'm just trying to be a good neighbor."

Instantly deflated, I felt my body slump with disappointment. She'd changed her mind and was trying to defend herself. Perhaps it had been the shocked reaction on Jake's face that had done it, or perhaps she was simply having second thoughts about the idea of hanging out with me.

I knew I couldn't really blame her. After all, he was the big, muscly kid of the grade. The one with the perfect mop of dark hair that seemed to stay in place in that cool way I always envied. He was the one that everyone looked up to, all the girls included. How could I possibly compete? Especially being the awkward weirdo freak that Jake was making me out to be.

When his cheeky grin returned, the one that usually managed to get him what he wanted, I decided that I had no hope.

"Maybe you should come and sit next to me before you get a bad reputation. It's your first week after all and you don't want to ruin your image." He kept grinning at her, waiting for her to make a move.

When Tess didn't budge and remained quietly in her seat, he was forced to continue. He was not used to people refusing him and in a last-ditch effort, he let loose with the one thing that he thought would be sure to work. All it did though was make me angrier than ever.

"Haven't you heard about his mom yet? She's some type of

weirdo hippie, calls herself a psychic. It's no wonder he's such a loser. You really ought to move. I'd hate to see that crazy stuff rub off on you!"

Dreading Tess's response, I couldn't bring myself to look at her. I was not at all sure how she'd react to his comments. Would she stand up and follow him, after offering me some lame apology? Or would she remain where she was? I had no idea.

With an intense heat bubbling inside my head, I watched stone-faced as Jake walked back to his table of friends and began sniggering and laughing, pointing at me and making me out to be the butt of his cruel joke.

His tray of food was right there in front of him and almost subconsciously, I concentrated my effort on one lone glass of chocolate milk. I could not resist. This time he had gone too far. The anger I was feeling had gone beyond my control and although I was aware of the power erupting inside me, I was helpless to stop it.

The glass and the tray began to shake. Jake was looking at me, smiling and laughing, along with the herd of followers who sat alongside him. Just like sheep, they copied his every move and if he thought the situation was funny, then they did too.

The glass on the tray in front of him began to move. At first, it was a slight wobble but then it shook harder. I looked on in fascination, as it continued to vibrate; right there, right under his nose. But he was so busy mocking me that he didn't even notice.

From my seat a short distance away, I could see his mouth move. I watched his lips as he spoke and laughed and sniggered out loud. I watched the roll of his eyes and the movement of his hands as he continued with his put-downs and mean comments; every single loud word directed towards me.

Gradually, the glass shook some more. Just a little at a time the vibration increased. But still, it had not caught his eye. So absorbed in his mockery and laughter, he sat there thriving on the attention of his friends.

Time seemed to tick on, almost in slow motion as I sat there watching. Watching and concentrating and focusing. Then, with a shattering blast, the glass exploded.

Squeals and screams could be heard as kids jumped back in fright. But mostly, the splash of brown milky liquid along with small chunks of glass were thrust all over Jake. And the look of astonishment on his face as he stared down at the chocolate milk dripping in pools around him, was almost worth the abuse and humiliation he had just made me suffer.

"Oh, my gosh, what just happened?" Tess exclaimed loudly beside me. "That sounded like a bomb going off."

Well aware that he was extremely lucky I hadn't done something more than just shatter the glass, I sat silently alongside her, taking in the scene in front of us. A bit of broken glass and a large spattering of chocolate milk didn't seem worthy of the punishment he truly deserved.

Tess however, was staring in Jake's direction, a concerned

look on her face. She seemed to have this 'caring thing' going on but to waste it on him was pointless in my opinion.

"He probably knocked it over on purpose." I finally replied. "Anything for attention. He sure made a mess though!"

Tess stared in silence and I could not help my next remark. "If he was hurt it's his own fault. He deserves everything that's coming to him!"

Frowning, she looked towards me and stared. She was not sure how to respond and when I noticed her expression become more curious, I decided to let the subject drop.

After unleashing myself on Jake, the last thing I wanted was for her to become suspicious. That was something I definitely wanted to avoid. My self-defense mechanism was something I never talked about. Only my mother knew my deep dark secret. It was one of the main reasons I wanted to contact my father so badly. I was desperate to know if he had that same power and if he was willing to teach me to control it. Although right then, I was not sorry in the slightest about what had just happened.

I just hoped that Tess still wanted to hang out. After what Jake had said about me, I half expected she would change her mind. And right then, I had no idea what she was thinking.

When the bell signaled the end of lunch break, it gave me no time to find out. Forced to stand and join the throng of kids heading back to class, I could do nothing except follow along behind the mass of students.

Samantha had grabbed hold of Tess and I tried to listen in on their conversation as they walked. The fact that 'poor' Jake was not only drenched with milk but could have been badly hurt, was all Samantha could talk about. But I didn't want to think about Jake or about what had just happened.

For the remainder of the afternoon, I struggled to concentrate at all. Barely comprehending a word that came out of my teacher's mouth, I tuned out completely from her monotonous voice and focused on something else entirely.

But instead of Minecraft or League of Legends or any of the other computer games that I usually thought about in place of the teacher's boring lessons, my mind was filled with thoughts of my new neighbor; the pretty girl who had moved in next door.

And until the final bell rang, I found it impossible to think of anything else.

Payback...

I was satisfied with what had happened to Jake during the lunch break earlier that day. Even though a small part of me wondered if I'd gone too far, I was convinced that he had brought it on himself and that he totally deserved it.

Besides that, I really had no control once my anger got the best of me. It did not happen often but when it did, I was unable to stop myself.

The surprising thing was that the Jake episode had happened in public and that in itself was unusual. There was only one other time that I'd let loose in front of an audience. That was when I was a little kid and threw a temper tantrum in a toy store over a game I wasn't allowed to have. But apart from that, every other incident had occurred at home with only my mom there to witness my outburst.

I distinctly remember the day in the shopping center so long ago. It was just after my dad had left us. I'm not sure if that was what caused me to act out, but when my mom refused to buy what I wanted, I was overcome with a sudden rage. The overhead lights that hung from the ceiling above began to flicker on and off and I felt this incredible throbbing in my head. Out of the blue, toys and other items started falling off the shelves in front of us.

After that, everything seemed to go black, and then all I remember is my mom shaking me and yelling at me to stop.

Ever since then, nothing like that has ever happened, not in public anyway. There were definitely times when I was tempted, but until Jake started with his abuse at school, I guess nothing else had pushed me to the point of no return, which was what I called it. Once overcome with that fog of anger, I found it very difficult to control myself.

Luckily when the Jake incident happened, Tess was sitting at my side. When I caught her glancing down at my clenched fists, and saw the frown she was directing towards me, I was forced to get myself under control. There was no way I wanted her to suspect that I might be the culprit. No one knew my secret and I needed to keep it that way.

Even though it had been a close call, it was still worthwhile. The look on Jake's face when the chocolate milk sprayed all over him was priceless. That was one image I was definitely going to keep fresh in my mind.

Ever since that lunch break, I was feeling better than I'd felt in a long time. But I knew there was also another reason for my change in mood. And I was sure it was what had lifted my spirits the most.

I had a new neighbor but it was not just any old neighbor, she was the girl of my dreams. Most people wouldn't expect it, but I did sometimes dream about having a girlfriend one day. Not that I really believed it would ever happen. After all, who would want to be the girlfriend of a mind freak?

But then Tess had shown up and not only was she actually nice to me, but she was also really pretty. The picture of her smiling face had been in my head all afternoon. And when I spotted her at the locker area after school, I felt a sudden case of extreme nerves. Or maybe it was just that I was excited to see her. I wasn't sure which, but whatever it was, it felt good.

When I noticed her, I happened to be shoving books inside my locker. But I pretended I didn't know she was there. Too shy to actually acknowledge her, I hoped more than anything that she'd say something to me instead. I also hoped that her invitation to go to her house after dinner was still on offer.

And then I saw Jake. Or rather, I heard him. His loud voice as he strutted down the corridor could be heard by everyone. He was the type of kid who always wanted to be noticed and that afternoon was no exception.

Of course, he had spotted Tess as well and as I watched from the corner of my eye, I could see that he was making a beeline towards her. It was obvious that he was not going to give up where she was concerned.

"Hey Tess, I know it's only your second day so you probably haven't heard about the school disco coming up in a couple of weeks. It's going to be really cool and you won't know too many people so you can hang out with me and my friends if you like."

"Thanks," she said in reply, as she closed her locker door. I guessed by her one-word response that she was a bit surprised with his up-front comment. The guy had only just met her and he was practically asking her out.

Pretending that I was searching through my locker, I was

able to stay where I was without them noticing me. But at the same time, I kept one eye on the scene going on just a short distance away.

"Yeah, it'll be fun," Jake persisted, obviously hoping for a more detailed reply from Tess. "I can introduce you to some of my friends tomorrow if you like."

"Okay, thanks," she repeated again as she began to walk away.

Jake, who had obviously expected a lot more enthusiasm, stepped into her path, preventing her from going further. "We hang out in the courtyard, so I'll meet you there in the morning. Make sure you get to school early so we have some time before the bell."

I glimpsed Tess nodding her head, but it was a half-hearted nod and I could tell that she didn't really mean it.

Then she spotted me and I instantly caught sight of her friendly smile.

"Hey, Sam. Are you still coming over tonight?"

I wasn't sure if I was imagining it, but I could feel every pair of eyes staring in my direction. There were several kids hanging around the locker area and I suspected they had all been as interested as me to watch Jake in action. But they had certainly not expected what they'd just seen and heard. And especially not with me involved.

Feeling my face flush a bright red, I closed my locker door and gulped. With so many pairs of eyes on me, I felt more awkward than ever.

"Aah, yeah," I stammered quietly, "Yeah, I'm still coming."

While I was over the moon that she still wanted to hang out, I could not help the uncomfortable sensation I was feeling. There were so many kids staring and to make matters even worse, Jake stood right beside Tess watching things unfold. And by his look of disbelief, I could easily imagine what was going through his head.

Is she for real? Is she seriously thinking of hanging out with that loser? This is a joke!

Unable to keep his thoughts to himself, he blurted out loudly, "I don't think it's a good idea to be hanging out with him, Tess. His mom's a witch, remember? You might end up being turned into a frog."

Chuckling out loud at his own stupid joke, the previous look of annoyance had turned to a smug grin, which grew even wider at the sound of the laughter around him. His followers were clearly enjoying the entertainment and stood waiting to see what would happen next.

But I was not interested in giving them the satisfaction they were after. What good would it do anyway? He was so much bigger than me, there was no way I would ever win a fight. And besides that, I did not want to make a fool of myself in front of Tess. The others, I couldn't care less about, but as far as Tess was concerned, her opinion was important.

Choosing to ignore him, I turned to walk away. What I didn't expect to see was Tess following in my wake. She appeared to have also chosen the avoidance tactic as the best option and had quickened her step to keep up.

Jake, obviously unhappy with the situation, made one more attempt and it was this comment that led to what happened next.

"Make sure you show Tess your crystal ball. FREAK! I'm sure she'll love it."

At the sound of the loud laughter behind me, I turned around. I wasn't sure if it was his words or the fact that I was the butt of his joke again, that upset me the most. Or perhaps, it was the total embarrassment I was feeling in front of the incredible new girl who seemed to be taking an interest in me.

Maybe it was a mixture of all three things. But whatever the reason, I welcomed the sudden tension in my brain, the familiar heat that was making me flush an even brighter red. Because in the very next second, the locker door that was right beside Jake's egotistical head, flung abruptly open, slamming roughly into his face.

"That'll teach him," I mumbled quietly as I turned towards the nearest exit.

Unable to help the smirk that had formed on my own face, I headed towards the bus stop to catch my bus, with Tess hurrying along behind me.

Jake...

Forcing away all thoughts of Jake, I concentrated on the girl sitting on the seat to my right. Even though there were kids sniggering around us, wondering why she'd even choose to talk to me, let alone sit alongside me on the bus, it was as though Tess managed to block them all out. She pretended she couldn't hear what they were saying and took no notice of their presence around us. And that meant more to me than anything.

"I'm not worried about them," she whispered, indicating the kids behind us. "I can make up my own mind about who I want to hang out with. And besides, there's no harm in being friends with my neighbor is there?"

Her reassuring grin was all I needed and I switched off from everything else except the smile on her face. She was the prettiest girl who had ever sat next to me on a bus, in fact, the only girl, and I decided right then to make the most of it. As was often the case for me, good things usually came to an end. I just hoped that this time might be an exception.

She was different to all the others and I thought that perhaps I'd finally made a real friend. But when she asked me about Jake, the tension in my body took an instant grip on my senses. The mere mention of his name had that immediate effect.

"Why do you let him speak to you like that?"

Her question was innocent enough but all it managed to do was make me angry inside.

Why *did* I let him talk to me the way he did? It was a fair enough question but I wasn't even certain that I knew the answer.

Sure, he was bigger than me.

Sure, he was tougher than me.

But was he smarter than me?

I knew that was a definite no.

At least that was one thing I had in my favor. Apart from that though, there wasn't much else.

Was he more popular?

Yes. Absolutely. He had a heap of friends, whereas I had none.

Was he sportier than me?

Definitely, yes. I sucked at sport.

I sighed as I looked towards her and shrugged my shoulders. Deep down, I did know the real reason. And I should have admitted it to myself a long time ago.

Jake was scary and intimidating and he had this power over me that I couldn't explain. While I knew I had my own power, the one I usually kept hidden and locked away, up until that day, it hadn't seemed to help me at all, at least not where he was concerned.

Although I knew I wasn't the only one that he bullied and tormented, I was definitely high on his list. And I suspected that with Tess around, his humiliating comments were likely to get worse.

The problem was, I was not sure how I would react to that.

And I was also not sure if I could control the inevitable.

It seemed right then that only time would tell.

The visit...

When I headed to her house that night after dinner, I felt more nervous than ever before. I was running late because it had taken me so long to get ready and I just hoped that I looked okay. I'd spent forever in the bathroom trying to get my hair to sit right. I'd smothered it in hair mousse which was something I didn't usually do. But that night I was desperate to make a good impression.

Jake had such a cool hairstyle and among other things, I'd always envied his hair. It looked so good on him and I wished mine would do the same. Instead, though, I was stuck with a mop of thick hair that just wanted to flop and do its own thing, regardless of how much mousse I used.

After what seemed like forever, all I ended up with was a greasy mess and I was forced to jump back in the shower and try to wash my hair clean again. Then I was faced with the next problem which was finding something decent to wear. I had never really worried too much about all the hand-me-downs that filled my cupboard, but that night, it was a big deal. For once, I wished that I at least owned a cool pair of jeans and maybe some Nikes like the majority of the other kids wore every day.

That sort of thing was beyond our budget though and on that night I had to make do with my regular pair of sneakers and a pair of faded black jeans that I dragged out of the laundry basket. They had that fresh washed smell and I was at least grateful that my favorite T-shirt was also clean. Even though it was a hand-me-down, the frayed edging on the sleeves somehow made it look better.

After one last glance in the mirror, I rushed out our front door, almost forgetting the cake that my mom had baked especially. She'd left it sitting on the kitchen bench for me to take over.

Luckily, at the last minute, I remembered and was able to run back inside to grab it. She definitely would not have been impressed to find it still sitting there when she arrived home later.

Her last words before she'd left to go out were, "Don't forget the cake!" She had even added icing to the top which was something she only did on special occasions. I just hoped that Tess and her parents liked banana and walnut cake as much as I did. It was not something I ever saw anyone else at school eat, although my mom made this one fairly often because I loved it so much.

With the almost forgotten cake in my hand, I climbed the steps leading to Tess's front door and took a deep breath in an effort to calm the thumping beat of my heart. I'd tried to convince myself that it was not necessary to get so worked up over visiting the neighbors. But that had done nothing to help.

There were a couple of issues involved and I could not seem to come to terms with either of them. Not only did a really pretty girl live in the house, but I had also never been inside before; even though I'd lived on the adjoining property my entire life.

The previous owner had been a grumpy old man who my mother tried to be friendly with on several occasions but had eventually given up on. He wanted to be left alone and was not at all interested in getting to know the people who lived next door.

My guess was that he'd heard about my mother's unusual occupation. The idea of a psychic lady living with her young kid in a run-down old house behind a thick screen of bush was too much for him. Just like the majority of our neighbors, he'd chosen to have as little to do with us as possible.

But when I stepped onto Tess's front veranda and the door swung wide open, I was instantly faced with her friendly smile and I knew instinctively that I had nothing to worry about.

Following her inside, I walked down a long hallway that led to a cozy and inviting living room at the back of the house. And as soon as I caught sight of her parents I could immediately see that they were as friendly and welcoming as Tess.

I also soon discovered that they absolutely loved banana and walnut cake and were very grateful for what they considered was an extremely kind gesture. After chatting for a while, I left them to follow Tess up to her room. As I climbed the stairs, I was pleased to overhear their comments about what a nice boy they thought I was.

At least I'd managed to make a good first impression which was something else that my mom had nagged me about before she left to go out.

I was curious about the interior of the house. It had remained hidden for so many years behind the screen of bush bordering our properties. It was such a mystery that I could not help but take the chance to glance every which way, as I headed up the stairs and along another corridor. There seemed to be rooms everywhere and each one was filled with a variety of cartons and boxes that as yet remained unpacked.

"This is a big house!" I exclaimed as I followed Tess to her room.

"Yeah, it is," Tess agreed as she walked along ahead of me. "The best thing about that is having so many bedrooms to choose from. Eventually, I decided on this one."

When she swung open the door of the last room at the end of the hallway, I realized instantly that she'd made a great choice. The room was huge and it had a large circular window at the far end.

There was something else about the room that immediately caught my attention. It faced directly towards my house and from that spot, I could see the light shining through the bushes to my own bedroom beyond. I'd left my bedside lamp on, and I could easily see its bright glow.

As well as that detail, there was so much more that caught my eye. Even though her family had only moved in a couple of days earlier, Tess's room was unpacked and completely organized; almost as though she'd been living there forever.

Her walls were covered in really cool posters of planets and galaxies and meteorites heading towards Earth. She had glow in the dark stars attached to her walls and ceiling, and I was sure they'd look awesome when the lights were switched off. I knew she was interested in astronomy, but it wasn't until I saw her room, that I realized how much. And then I spotted the telescope that she'd told me about. It was even more impressive than she'd made it out to be.

Moving towards it I asked her if I could take a look. By the size, it was obviously extremely powerful and I could hardly wait to try it out. With a quick grin, she nodded in agreement, eager to see what I thought. It only took one glance and I was hooked. The view of the night sky through that telescope was like nothing I'd ever seen before and I knew that I could easily have gazed through it for hours.

Because it was such a clear night, we could see endless numbers of stars but the best thing was definitely the moon. I'd stared at the moon on so many occasions from my own bedroom window in the past, but looking at it with the naked eye was absolutely no comparison to viewing it through a high-powered telescope. There was so much detail that could be seen, and I felt as though I could almost reach out and touch it.

When I thought about it later, I realized that looking through Tess's telescope while she talked about all the amazing things she had seen in space, was more fun than anything I'd done in a long time. Of course checking out the night sky was a pretty cool thing to do but what I enjoyed the most was just hanging out with Tess. I'd never really had too many friends and definitely never any close buddies who I could just spend time with. But by the time I left Tess's house later that night, I felt that I had actually made a real friend.

The nervous anticipation that had been sitting in the bottom of my stomach earlier that night had been replaced with an overwhelming excitement. It had all happened so quickly with very little effort at all, and when I made my way up to my own bedroom, I could feel the wide grin still stuck to my face.

The only things that ever usually got me excited were my computer games, in particular, the ones where I became the leader of an intense battle. The adrenalin that pumped through my veins during those times was something I didn't think I could experience anywhere else. But right then, as well as excitement, I noticed that I was feeling a different emotion, one that I was definitely not used to. And when I tried to analyze it, I decided that for the first time in a long time, I felt happy.

When I eventually climbed into bed and closed my eyes, her face was what remained in my mind. The fact that her parents also seemed to like me, just added to the mix. And not only had they said I could come over anytime, Tess had actually invited me for a movie night on the weekend as well.

We'd discovered that we both love science fiction films. For me, they are the best type of movie ever. Although, I'd probably even sit through a girlie movie if that was what she liked. It would be worth it just to hang out with her.

The idea of a really pretty girl living right next door who liked the same things as me was incredible. She was the coolest person I'd ever met and I could hardly wait for the following day so I could see her again.

As it turned out though, the next day did not go ahead as I'd imagined.

But I realized later that maybe I was expecting too much. After all, we had only just met and I guessed that a real friendship would take some time. I just hoped she would not end up being like all the others; all the mean kids who looked at me like I really was some type of weirdo freak.

But I soon found out that with Jake involved, that might be too much to ask for.

Disappointed...

The first person I noticed when I arrived at school the following day, of course, was Jake. He was in his usual spot with his usual crew of friends surrounding him. Just like bodyguards, they followed him everywhere he went. Not that he needed them. He did a good enough job of protecting himself and did not require a gang of loyal supporters sticking up for him. But then I guess that's what gave him his power and as usual, the confident smirk was stuck to his face as he sat there like some sort of King, watching over his domain.

Deciding to avoid him, I made my way to my usual place to wait for the bell to ring, the bell that signaled the start of class. That's when I spotted her. Walking along the pavement with Samantha Evans. They were headed towards a large group of girls nearby.

I sat watching from a distance, taking in the scene in front of me, well aware that Jake had also caught sight of her. All I could do though was stay in my secluded spot and try to hide from their view.

Jake made his way towards the group. He walked right up to them and I could easily hear his loud greeting.

"Hey girls. Watcha up to?"

As if by magic, they instantly turned towards him, their faces lit with welcoming smiles. Eager to have him join them, they shuffled along in order to make room for him to sit. Then, within seconds, all I could hear was their cheery laughter.

How did he do that? How was he able to approach a group like them, the prettiest girls in the grade, and just fit in? As I watched Tess's face break into a wide smile, I felt the jealousy ripple inside me. It was just a tremor at first but one I was struggling to control. And then the unexpected happened.

I have no idea why Tess suddenly looked in my direction. She must have felt me staring because I wasn't sure what else would have caused her to abruptly look my way. But when she did, we immediately made eye-contact.

Embarrassed that I'd been caught out, I glanced around, trying to pretend that I'd been staring at no one in particular, and then I heard her call my name.

"Sam! Sam!"

I could hear her voice, it was a friendly tone, trying to gain my attention. But I did not want her attention right then, not in front of so many kids, right there in the middle of the grassy area where everyone sat.

Forced to turn towards her, I found her waving and eagerly indicating for me to join her. She was actually expecting that I would stand and cross that void; with everyone watching, everyone including Jake. And then sit down amongst them as if it were a normal everyday thing for me to do.

When the others in her group caught on, that was when my embarrassed flush turned an even darker shade, and I was grateful at least, for the distance between us.

Unable to resist the opportunity, Jake began sniggering something or other, whispering to the girls as he continued glancing back at me. I couldn't hear his words, but I could easily imagine what he was saying. I was clearly the butt of his joke once again, and when they all broke into hysterical fits of laughter, I watched the smug grin light his face.

Everyone except Tess it seemed, was cracking up over whatever it was he'd shared. Although I could see that Tess wasn't amused, it did nothing to ease the deep flush of red that continued its steady journey down my cheeks and onto my neck and chest. As if I'd been torched by fire, I felt my body ignite and all I wanted to do was escape.

Quickly standing, I headed along the pavement towards our classroom, my gaze focused on the ground in front of me. And with each step I took, I felt a burning sensation from several pairs of eyes as they bored into my back.

When I slumped down in the safety of my seat alongside the classroom window, I could still feel the flush of shame on my cheeks and I busied myself at my desk, trying to occupy myself with some unfinished homework from the night before.

From the corner of my eye, I caught sight of Tess as she entered the classroom. But I kept my head down and didn't dare look her way. I was too ashamed and just wanted the ground to open up and swallow me.

For the remainder of the day, I hid away in the back of the library during break times, not even daring to venture outside. And when the bell rang at the end of the afternoon, I hurried to find a seat on the bus.

Although still ashamed over what had happened that morning, I secretly hoped that Tess would overlook it all and choose to sit next to me once more. I knew there was no way I could hang out with her at school if she continued to be friends with Samantha and the others, but because we lived next door to each other, at least I'd be able to spend time with her after school. If she still wanted to that was.

Then, to my dismay, I caught sight of her golden hair from the bus window, just as the bus was pulling away from the curb. When I turned in my seat to get a better view, I realized that she was heading down the street in the direction of the nearby shopping center, with Samantha and a few of the other girls.

Obviously, she would not be catching my bus home that afternoon but just as the bus gathered speed, I spotted Jake and a couple of his friends running to catch up with them.

A feeling of overwhelming disappointment took over. And for the remainder of the trip home, I focused on the scene I had just left behind. Images of the group hanging out together for the afternoon raced through my mind and I kicked the seat in front of me in frustration.

When the kid sitting there turned around and complained, I glared back at him, daring him to say another word. He opened his mouth to speak but then decided better of it and with a concerned frown turned back towards the front, obviously deciding it was better to keep quiet.

Just when I felt that I had something to look forward to, it was abruptly whipped away. That scenario seemed to be the story of my life. And when I walked into my bedroom I ignored my mother's nagging voice from downstairs reminding me to get on with my homework before going near the computer.

Slamming my bedroom door shut, I pushed the startup button and sat impatiently waiting for my computer screen to come to life.

With my hand on the mouse, I scrolled for my favorite game, the one with all the fighting and warfare, the one where I could be a leader and shine.

That was where I belonged. In front of a computer screen playing war games. And with a deep sigh, I prepared myself for battle.

Power...

When I crossed paths with Jake the following morning, I was at my locker searching for my Math textbook. It was something I should have taken home the day before so I could get my homework done, but Math homework was the last thing I'd felt like doing. That morning though, I knew our teacher would be checking to see who had completed the work and I was hoping to at least get some of the exercises done before the bell went.

Just as I reached for the book, I heard Jake's voice behind me. That loud confident drawl of his announcing his presence wherever he went, it could not be mistaken. Deciding it best to avoid any sort of eye-contact, I kept my eyes focused on the interior of my locker and waited for him to pass. But he had obviously decided there was fun to be had and as was usual for Jake, he could not pass up an opportunity.

Shoving past me as he walked by, his shoulder roughly nudged against my own, causing my head to bang into the open locker door.

"Oh, sorry Sam!" he smirked loudly, making sure everyone around him heard. "Hope I didn't hurt you!"

Chuckling loudly, he continued on his way. He'd had his little bit of fun, got the attention he wanted from the other kids who were milling around the area, and was clearly happy to keep going.

I could feel my blood begin to boil. I was sick of being made a fool of and I was sick of Jake. Without any thought or planning whatsoever, I focused on a long-handled, heavy looking wooden broom that happened to be leaning against the wall a little way down the corridor. It must have been left there by the janitor earlier that morning, but for me right then, it was just what I needed.

It took no effort at all to make that broom fall from its resting place onto the figure of the person passing by. The timing was perfect and the aim spot on. The broom fell heavily onto Jake's shoulder banging against his head with a loud whack.

"Ow!" I heard his moan from where I stood a little way down the hall, and every pair of eyes turned in his direction.

"Yes!" I whispered the word triumphantly to myself, unable to help the satisfied grin that had appeared on my face. It felt good, really good to get some pay-back.

Just as the broom connected with his head, Tess had appeared up ahead, probably making her way to her locker. And with a worried frown, she raced towards Jake to help him. From the spot where I stood, I could easily see the concern etched on her face.

"Jake, are you okay?" she asked, as she grabbed hold of the broom and laid it on the floor along the edge of the wall, out of the way.

"Yeah, I'm okay," he replied, standing up straighter and pretending that it hadn't hurt him at all.

But I caught his wounded glance as he looked quickly around, obviously embarrassed about who else might have witnessed the scene. The feeling of embarrassment was something he was not used to and I enjoyed being the one to watch *his* uncomfortable reaction for a change. We briefly made eye-contact and rather than avoiding his gaze, this time I stared back, waiting for him to look away first.

The sense of satisfaction, although minor in the scheme of things, felt good and I grinned to myself at the thought of the heavy broom hitting him so abruptly. What I hadn't planned on though was for Tess to fuss over him. That was the last thing I wanted to see. And to make matters worse, she then continued on down the hallway, deep in conversation and right by his side.

Feeling the anger inside me beginning to surface once more, I slammed my locker door closed with a bang. And with my Math book in my hand, I turned in the opposite direction in search of a quiet place to do my homework.

As the day went on, I noticed Tess by Jake's side on several times. It seemed that he'd paired up with her to do an in-class history project and when we were directed to the computer lab for research, he quickly made his way to her side.

I'd barely said a word to Tess since my visit to her house and the one time she had approached me, a friendly smile on her face, Jake had appeared from nowhere and taken over in his usual overpowering manner. With a smirk in my direction, he'd grabbed hold of Tess's hand and dragged her away to sit with his group of friends. It seemed to me that with him around, I didn't have a chance. But I was unwilling to give up so easily.

During our lunch break, I spotted Jake and his friends all hanging out together with Tess, Samantha, and the other girls. I could tell that already, they'd formed a close-knit group and their laughter and loud chatter could be heard across the grassy area where everyone was sitting.

Their happy little scene caused my skin to prickle with disgust. Normally I would just ignore them all but the sight of Tess surrounded by that jerk and his followers made me angry. Jake didn't deserve to have Tess as a friend and that was what hurt the most. Why everything always seemed to work out for kids like him was something I could not understand and the longer I sat there watching, the angrier I became.

Once again, I felt the rise of an intense heat. Like a raging fire, it was gaining strength and power inside me. Noticing a couple of kids kicking a football nearby, I found that I was unable to control my actions and almost trance-like, I stood and took a few steps towards them. Concentrating carefully, I focused on the ball just as it hit its peak in the sky then began its downward descent. But rather than falling into the hands of the boy who was waiting to catch it, it took a sudden sharp turn.

Jake's head was the target I was aiming for, and once again my accuracy was spot on. Bypassing everyone else in the group and heading directly towards the middle of his forehead, the ball connected perfectly. Proud of my aim, I grinned widely as I watched him rock backward, the force of the blow almost causing him to overbalance completely.

Gasping in surprise and shock, he rubbed his forehead and stood, glaring towards the boys who had been kicking the ball.

"Hey! What do ya think ya doing?" he bellowed loudly.

The two kids stood open-mouthed and speechless, unable to comprehend what had just happened.

To me, the entire scene was magical and I felt like an onlooker witnessing something quite remarkable. The sense of accomplishment was too good to ignore and I could not help but laugh out loud.

My excited reaction quickly faded away when I noticed

Tess's curious and confused expression. She was looking towards me and obviously wondering what had caused the ball to collide with Jake.

Quickly moving away from the scene, I kept my head down and tried to make myself invisible. Perhaps I'd gone too far, but I'd been unable to help it.

Jake deserved everything he got and nothing was going to convince me otherwise.

My escape route led right past where he was standing and I made the mistake of glancing his way, just for the briefest of moments.

I'd been reveling in my victory and was keen to check out the damage. When I spotted the red mark and an angry egg-shaped lump that was already forming on his forehead, I could not help but stare a little longer.

This, of course, was the wrong thing to do. Two embarrassing incidents in one day was clearly too much for Jake to deal with and he glared at me and let fly.

"What are you lookin' at? Weirdo Freak!"

Instantly the attention had reverted to me. And Jake, with his need to move the humiliation onto someone else, continued with his abuse.

"Watch out little boy. Or I'm gonna getcha. Yeah, you and your psychic weirdo mom. Haha! Talk about weirdos!"

Laughing loudly at his own attempt at humor, he glanced around, encouraging his supporters to join in. But I could not take my eyes from him. He had overstepped the mark once again. Humiliating me was one thing but bringing my mom into the mix was another, and the heat inside my head abruptly reached boiling point.

79

The sensation became more intense and I was forced to rub my head to try to ease the pressure that was bursting at my temples.

Ignoring the pain, I looked quickly around and spotted the perfect weapon. When I thought about it later, I realized how uncanny it was that Jake happened to be standing in that exact spot.

The crackling sound of the tree branch above his head was loud and clear and I watched in fascination as it gradually broke away from the trunk.

Almost in slow motion, it seemed to make its descent, just like the steady fall of the football a short while earlier. And a little at a time it headed towards the target below. But Jake, intent on his outburst and making as big a scene as possible in front of the growing number of onlookers, seemed oblivious to what was going on.

Moving back out of harm's way, I ignored his taunts but continued to focus on the tree branch directly above his head. Then, as if suddenly aware of what I was staring at, he looked up and froze, just as the branch broke clean away from the tree.

I watched in awe as he bolted quickly out of reach and I could clearly see why he was such a valued member of the football team. Regardless of his size and bulk, he could move at lightning speed and that was definitely what saved him.

"Jake!!!"

I heard the cries of several kids calling his name in warning as they watched the scene unfold. And I also noticed the surprised and shocked reactions of every person there, Tess included.

As several of them rushed towards him, I made a fast exit and disappeared from sight. The heat inside my head was beginning to subside, but the adrenalin pumping through my veins was causing my heart to continue pounding wildly in my chest.

Gulping in a deep breath of much-needed air, I put my head down and continued on my way towards the classroom and the last session of the day.

The feeling of satisfaction in my gut filled me with a pride I knew I didn't deserve. But the scene I had just left behind had created a power that I had never before fully appreciated.

Despair...

For the remainder of the afternoon, I didn't dare make eye-contact with anyone. My gaze went from the teacher's notes on the board to the page of my open book and I concentrated on copying down the information, glad to have something to focus on. As soon as the afternoon bell went, I left quickly for the bus. But once again, Tess was nowhere to be seen.

It occurred to me that I might never get a chance to see her again, except maybe from a distance. And when I eventually reached the safety of my bedroom and dumped my bag on the floor beside my desk, I stared longingly through the bushes towards her house, where I could see glimpses of the exterior.

Wondering if she was hanging out with Jake again that afternoon, I wandered around my room, frustrated and annoyed. The heat inside my head was bubbling again and I sat down at my desk, trying to control the angry feeling that was winding through my senses.

It wasn't fair. Every time I had a chance to pay him back, it seemed to backfire with just about every girl in our class running to Jake with sympathy.

"Are you alright, Jake?"

"Jake, are you okay?"

"Oh my gosh, Jake, you're so lucky you weren't hurt!"

And then there was the admiration...

"Jake! That was amazing."

"Jake! You are so fast!"

I pictured the faces of the girls who constantly ran to his aid.

Jake, Jake, Jake. The sound of his name ringing in my head made me cringe with contempt. And focusing on an empty glass sitting on my desk, I watched as it lifted into the air and flew across the room, smashing against the wall with a loud crash.

In disgust, I looked at the mess on the floor, knowing full well that I'd have to clean it up before my mom arrived home. Otherwise, there would be questions asked. And that was something I wanted to avoid.

Glancing around the room in frustration, I concentrated on other items sitting on my desk. First a couple of pens and a notebook, then an abandoned History textbook. After that, a flashlight that sat on a shelf. Before I knew it, I was surrounded by several random items hovering in midair around me.

In the past, there had been long periods where I had not used my powers at all but lately, I seemed to be fighting the urge more and more often. Causing a heavy tree branch to fall down was definitely the most powerful thing I'd ever attempted, and probably the most dangerous. But my pent-up anger had made me lose all control.

As I sat there, deep in thought over the events of the afternoon, I decided to test my powers further. Usually, I could only move one thing at a time but without realizing it, I'd managed to collect several items at once and keep them afloat with barely any effort at all.

Focusing a little more, I began to lift each individual item higher into the air and zoom them all quickly across the room, stopping just short of the wall. It looked pretty cool and I grinned widely to myself as I attempted some soaring and diving of pens, notepads and glass containers, watching with fascination as they zoomed around me.

Then I decided to include heavier items. The memory of the falling tree branch and the power I'd felt was still clear in my head and I wanted to experience it again. Getting off my chair, I stood alongside the window to allow more room around me. From there, I watched as my chair floated into space and joined the other flying objects.

Grinning with satisfaction, I took in the scene. The knowledge that I had the power to create such a scene filled me with a pride I desperately needed right then; anything to make me feel good about myself.

But then, a sudden movement outside the window happened to catch my eye. It had been a quick flash that caught my attention and I whipped around to stare down into the garden and the overgrown backyard below.

The curtain was drawn open so I had a clear view of the entire area. As I scanned the thick bush that bordered the edge of the yard, I noticed a flash of blonde hair and a figure quickly retreating back along the track in the opposite direction.

The green T-shirt she was wearing allowed her to blend in with the surroundings and it had taken a moment for me to spot her. But the glow of her hair in the afternoon sunlight was unmistakable, and I knew without a doubt that the person lurking there had been Tess.

With a sinking feeling wallowing deeper and deeper in the depths of my stomach, I stood staring from my window. Rather than the joy I should have felt at the thought of her coming to visit, I was overcome with panic.

How long had she been there and how much had she seen? Not only had my stomach dropped to the lowest point possible, every item that had been floating around me had also crashed to the floor, each one with a loud smashing sound as it hit the hard wooden floor.

But it was not the mess nor the broken containers and bits of glass that I was concerned about. My problem was Tess and the fact that she had more than likely discovered my secret.

With a deep intense fear, one that was quickly engulfing me, I pulled the curtains closed and sat down on my bed in despair.

Book 2

Discovery

The sighting...

At first, I was sure it had to be my imagination running wild in the way that it so often did. Right then, as I stood frozen to my spot amidst the row of dense bush that separated Sam's garden from mine, I could think of no other explanation. Convinced that the scene could not be real, I rubbed my eyes to clear the crazy image away. But still it remained and nothing would shake it from view. In fact, the more I blinked, the clearer it became.

My fascination turned to awe as I stood transfixed and immobile, watching the scene take place in front of me. Sam's bedroom window was open wide and the curtains were drawn, giving me an unobstructed view of the various objects zipping and zooming around the room. That in itself was strange enough. But the image of him standing calmly by while an odd assortment of items whipped past him, often narrowly missing him by mere inches, was the most bizarre thing I had ever witnessed. In real life anyway.

I was so mesmerized by what was going on that at first I didn't catch the sudden turn of his head. I had no idea what caused him to abruptly glance out the window in my direction. But when I thought about it later, I felt sure that somehow he was able to sense my presence. I also decided that perhaps he was psychic just like his mother.

But at that moment, none of those thoughts were important. What mattered right then was the fact that I was not camouflaged by the surrounding trees as I'd previously thought. Instead, Sam was completely aware that I was standing there, wide-eyed and confused as I stared directly towards him. Being caught out, watching something I knew

I was not meant to see, caused a sudden ball of fear to form in the pit of my stomach. And without another moment's hesitation, I turned and raced back to the safety of my house.

Ignoring the scrape of branches on the bare skin of my arms, my need to escape spurred me on and I pushed through the undergrowth towards the privacy of my garden. Without stopping for breath, I made my way quickly across the freshly cut grass and up the steps leading to our front door.

It wasn't until I entered the house and slammed the door shut behind me that I paused for a moment, my heart thumping in my chest. Then, making sure that the lock was firmly in place, I took the stairs two at a time, desperate to reach my bedroom.

My head spun as I pictured once more in my mind, the scene I had just left behind. Glancing towards my open window, I rushed to close it. Sam was just on the other side of the tall trees that separated our properties, and only a short stretch of garden lay between us.

Drawing the curtains closed in an attempt to form a barrier, I slumped down on my bed, my heart still racing wildly. The boy who I thought I'd come to know was not at all what he seemed. Instead, I'd just discovered that the kid who everyone at school had warned me about, actually did possess some type of supernatural power. At least that was how it appeared. I had witnessed the scene with my own eyes and there was no other reasonable explanation.

He'd been labeled a weird freak whose mom was a psychic witch of some kind. All the stories I'd heard came flooding back. Perhaps all the rumors were true and behind closed doors, all kinds of strange things went on in the ramshackle property next door. And if that really were the case then what else were Sam and his mom capable of?

As I sat on my bed, propped up against the wall by one of the colored cushions that sat decoratively over the quilt, I clutched tightly to my favorite. It was heart-shaped and covered in a soft velvety fabric. The bright purple tone created a vivid contrast amongst the other colors and its soft texture gave me comfort as I sat there deep in thought.

Finally, the beat of my heart had slowed to a steady rhythm and I was able to think more logically, with the answers coming to me one by one.

Every strange thing that had taken place, every weird, unexplainable event that I'd witnessed since moving next door to Sam, had been caused by him. The accidents and near misses surrounding Jake, the objects mysteriously falling into Jake's path, the glass of milk that had suddenly exploded into a thousand pieces and splashed all over him, and worst of all the fallen tree branch that Jake miraculously escaped from; at last there was a clear explanation for every single detail.

Sam was to blame for everything. I was sure of it.

At that moment, the anxious sensations that were swirling inside me rapidly turned to alarm.

Sam...

When I arrived at school the following day, my eyes darted in every direction looking for Tess. I'd barely slept the night before, unable to get her out of my thoughts and she was still foremost in my mind.

The image of her shocked expression the previous afternoon had been on constant rewind and I was unable to escape it. The moment I'd so carelessly looked out my bedroom window and glimpsed a flash of the golden highlights in her hair, my stomach had dropped. It was an instant dead weight that made me feel ill and the sensation of nausea was still with me as I headed into the school grounds.

It's a disaster! How could I have let it happen? There's no way she'll even talk to me anymore, let alone be my friend.

The thoughts swirled relentlessly through my brain. And with each step I took, I searched for her, desperate to know one way or another, what the outcome would be.

That was when I spotted her. She was standing amongst a group of kids. Jake, of course, was alongside her and as soon as she saw me, she froze. But it was as though the entire group did the same. And each and every pair of eyes darted my way.

They all know! They all know I'm a freak.

Sick with fear, I put my head down and quickened my pace, desperate to get as far away from their stares as possible.

Why, oh why did I go to school? How could I have been so stupid!

The question haunted me as I made my way up the steps and into the building in search of a place to hide.

I could easily have avoided school that day. All I had to do was catch a different bus after leaving the house that morning. My mom would never have known. I'd certainly skipped school enough times before and got away with it. But instead of finding somewhere to hide, a place of my own away from prying eyes and kids suspecting me of being some type of alien freak, I'd climbed aboard the school bus. Then, of course, I'd ended up in the one place I needed to escape from.

I was such a fool. That fact seemed so clear right then. But even though I knew how much of an idiot I was, I was also aware of the real reason I'd decided to go to school.

It was to see her.

To see Tess and find out for sure if she was going to desert me, isolate me in the way I'd become familiar with in the days and years before her arrival. No friends, constantly hanging out on my own with only my computer games for company, and back to my loser status.

Deep down, I knew the answer. But regardless, I'd maintained a small glimmer of hope that everything would sort itself out and that Tess and I would carry on as we were.

I heard her words in my head. It was a fantasy that I desperately wanted to become real.

Hey Sam! I saw a heap of stuff floating around your room! That's so cool! Can you show me how you do it?

Haha! As if!

What a joke! What a ridiculous joke!

It could happen in the recesses of my mind, the place I go to hide away from the world. But definitely not in reality. Not in my reality, anyway.

As I raced up the stairs to disappear into the darkened gloom of the corridors beyond, the anxiety in the pit of my stomach worsened.

Tess...

I saw Sam before he saw me. From the corner of my eye, I caught sight of his familiar green bomber jacket, the one that he loved to wear. And although his eyes were downcast, and his hair fell in waves across his face hiding it from view, I knew it was him. I would recognize that figure anywhere.

His eyes darted quickly from side to side before returning in the direction of the pavement at his feet. But he continued insistently on his way, as if on a mission of some sort; a call to keep going, to keep moving forward.

And then all of a sudden he glanced my way. It was as though he could feel me staring. It was like a magnetic force of some kind that caused him to look towards me.

He stared back only for a moment. It was long enough though, for me to catch the intensity of his facial expression. My breath caught in my throat as he passed by, his shoulders slumped in despair and sadness. But it was more than that. At first, I couldn't quite decipher it, and then almost instinctively, I knew. It was fear. I was sure of it.

But why would he be afraid? Surely I was the one who had the right to be frightened. I was the one who had witnessed the bizarre scenario through his bedroom window; objects zooming at lightning speed around his room as he stood calmly by, watching them float and hover in front of him. To him, it was probably the most natural thing in the world. But for me, it was something else. Something I was not at all sure how to deal with.

Before glimpsing his uncertain look, I'd convinced myself to stay away from him. To take notice of all the warnings I'd been given and keep my distance. I'd begun to believe that maybe he was a freak of some sort; a dangerous, crazy weirdo, capable of strange powers and who knew what else. But all of a sudden I wasn't so sure. Perhaps I had the wrong idea.

As I stood there, watching him disappear into the crowd of kids surrounding the entrance to the school building, I was overcome with a sudden curiosity; a need to know more about the mysterious boy who lived next door. The voices of my friends became a dull drone in my head and my thoughts focused on Sam.

Making a split second decision, I decided that I would find a time to confront him, to actually ask him what was going on. Surely he owed me an explanation. And I was determined that he would give me one. In the meantime, his secret would remain just that. A secret that I was beginning to think, only I knew about.

Pushing my fears and doubts aside allowed an abrupt tingling of excitement to work its way through me. Somehow I knew that my life was about to change. But whether that was a good thing or not, I had no idea.

The search...

There were moments throughout the day where I caught Sam glancing towards me, but each time we made eye contact he turned quickly away. During lunch breaks, he was nowhere to be seen and although I looked briefly around for him, I couldn't find him anywhere.

I could barely wait for the day to end and when the final bell rang, I joined the throng of kids in the hallway heading for their lockers. Losing sight of Sam, I ran for the bus, hoping to grab a seat next to him. That would have been the perfect opportunity for a chance to talk but when I boarded the steps and headed down the aisle, there was no sign of him anywhere. When the bus pulled away from the curb and still he had not appeared, I sighed with frustration. He was avoiding me, I was sure of it. But I was determined to find out what I could.

As soon as the bus slowed to a stop outside my house, I made my way quickly down the steps and along the pavement towards the front door. Closing it firmly behind me, I bypassed the kitchen which was where I usually headed as soon as I arrived home after school. That afternoon, however, food and hunger were the last things on my mind.

When I reached my bedroom, I threw my school bag onto the floor in its usual spot alongside my desk and sat down at my computer. I would confront Sam as soon as I found the chance, but in the meantime, I wanted to do some investigating of my own. That entire day I'd been unable to concentrate on anything except Sam's secret. I could not let it go and was anxious to learn more.

Going straight to Google, I typed in the words...*is it possible to move objects with your mind...*

I saw instantly that there was a great deal of information on this subject and clicked on the first link that appeared on the list. The very first sentence I read informed me that the technique was called telekinesis. It was a term I'd never heard of before and at first, I wasn't even sure how to pronounce it. But the more I read, the more I learned about this phenomena, and sitting back in my chair, my mind ticked over with doubt. If what I was reading were true, then Sam was simply a magician of some sort, practicing magic tricks and that was all; he did not have supernatural powers at all.

According to the scientific evidence on the screen in front of me, telekinesis, the ability to move things with a person's mind, was impossible. The report claimed that over the span of many centuries various people including famous magicians had managed to fake this skill. Apparently, they were so clever that they were able to fool their audience every time. But it was later discovered that hidden wires and magic tricks had been used.

In order to prove that telekinesis was impossible, scientists had conducted a variety of experiments and investigations and were able to provide evidence that trickery had been used in each case.

I thought back to the scene I witnessed the day before which had certainly seemed real enough. But I was beginning to think that it actually was just a case of my over-active imagination convincing me that all the rumors about Sam were true. What if he had simply been practicing magic tricks? And from my spot in the garden, I couldn't see all the wires and bits and pieces that were hidden from view?

Perhaps I really did have it all wrong!

Then I remembered his odd behavior at school that day. Why was he avoiding me and acting so strangely? It just didn't make sense.

Going back to the google search bar, I decided to continue looking. There was lots of information and I was interested to see what all the other websites had to say. I knew what I had seen the day before. If it was simply a magic act, then Sam was very good at it. Because it definitely seemed real to me.

That was when I discovered pages and pages claiming that telekinesis did in fact, exist. According to what I found on every other website, telekinesis was described as a psychic phenomenon made possible by mind power. There were even instructions and YouTube videos demonstrating the steps involved; included were step by step instructions explaining the process. I wasn't sure if it was possible for regular people to learn the skill but when I considered the fact that Sam's mom worked as a psychic, this new information seemed to fit. If his mother really was psychic then surely it was possible that he may have psychic powers as well.

Moving towards the nearby window, I stood for a moment, looking out in the direction of his house. Deep in thought, I pictured Sam once again in his room, with objects of various shapes and sizes flying around him. My mind raced with the possibility that Sam was telekinetic; that telekinesis was his secret, the one that he'd tried to keep hidden from everyone.

All of a sudden, I heard his mom's voice. It carried across the treetops and into my room. She was calling out to Sam and asking him to come downstairs for something to eat. I did not hear a response, but obviously, he'd made it home. His mom had either picked him up or he had walked home from school and was now more than likely upstairs in his attic bedroom.

Spontaneously and without giving the idea any further thought, I raced out of my bedroom, down the stairs and past my own mother who stared at me in surprise.

"You're home!" she exclaimed. "I didn't hear you come in."

When I moved towards the front door and reached for the handle, swinging the door open wide, I called back a quick explanation.

"I'm just going next door to see Sam. I won't be long!"

And without waiting for a reply, I ran across the front garden in the very same direction that I'd escaped from just the afternoon before.

Once again, my heart was thumping in my chest but this

time it was not caused by fear. Rather, it was excitement that spurred me on as I pushed my way along the overgrown track, moving branches aside to clear my path.

And when I knocked on Sam's front door, I waited impatiently for someone to answer.

The visit…

When Sam's mom came to the door, she greeted me with a warm smile.

"Tess!" she exclaimed, "What a lovely surprise! You must be here to visit Sam!"

"Yes, I am," I replied, smiling back. "Is it okay if I come in?"

I'd only met her briefly once before. It was the day that we moved into our house and I had to rescue my dog, Jasper from their garden. On that occasion, she was just as friendly. And once again, I noticed her hippy style clothing. This time, she was wearing bright purple pants and a colorful floral top. A large silver pendant buckled the wide leather belt around her waist and it matched the silver and leather entwined band that was wrapped around her wrist. Her hair curled around her face in long dark waves and her almond-shaped eyes seemed to sparkle when she smiled.

My impression when I first met her, was that she was like no one I had ever met before, and once again I thought how different she was to my own mother. This time, I took in her pretty features and youthful appearance, realizing she was actually quite young, very young in fact, to have a son Sam's age. Her warm smile and sparkling eyes made me feel welcome. And I took an instant liking to her.

"Come in, come in!" she said, beckoning me to follow her into a living room crowded with an odd assortment of mismatched furniture. "Sam didn't tell me you were coming over. But it's perfect timing because I'm about to take a cake out of the oven!"

"I hope you like banana and walnut cake!" she added, raising her eyebrows hopefully.

Nodding enthusiastically in response, I replied, "Oh yes, I love banana and walnut cake, especially yours!"

My mouth watered at the smell of the delicious aroma coming from the kitchen and I remembered the cake that Sam brought over when he came to visit me at my house. It was the tastiest banana cake I had ever tried. Even my mom had agreed that it was much better than the one she sometimes made and she was planning to ask Sam's mom for the recipe.

Glancing around the house as I followed behind her, I found there was so much to look at. I took in the cluttered space where I could see that every spare surface was topped with an assortment of trinkets, statues, and carvings of all shapes and sizes. Pictures, paintings, and wall hangings adorned just about every available spot on the wall. It was so different from my own home in every possible way.

My mother was a neat freak and everything had a place. In addition to that, my house was so uncluttered in comparison, with each room organized and tidy, every spare item packed away in cupboards or standing in place on various shelves.

I wouldn't call Sam's house untidy, it was just full of stuff. Everywhere I looked there seemed to be something to look at. It was quite clear that his mom was extremely different to my own mother in every possible way.

"Sam!" she called loudly, as she paused at the bottom of a winding staircase.

"Sam!" she repeated when there was no response.

I glanced upwards but all I could see was an endless set of stairs that wound around and around in a spiral, leading to the very upper level of the house.

"He's probably tuned into his computer games!" she exclaimed with a shake of her head. "When he's playing those, a bomb could go off and he wouldn't hear it."

I glanced towards the stairs once more but there was no movement whatsoever. In fact, not a sound could be heard and I wondered for a moment if he was actually at home.

"I need to rescue this cake from the oven," she added, pointing in the direction of the kitchen. "Why don't you just go on up. Follow the staircase all the way to the top. It's the attic bedroom. And please let him know I'm about to take a banana cake out of the oven. It's his favorite, and practically the only thing that will entice him from his room."

With that, she disappeared along a hallway and I was left standing alone at the bottom of the stairs. Staring silently, I looked up at the winding staircase in front of me. Feeling a sudden unease at my spontaneous decision to visit him uninvited, I hesitated for a moment before moving onto the first step.

I had no idea how Sam was going to react when he saw me. It wasn't as though he was expecting me at his door, and I wasn't at all sure I'd be welcome. Feeling like an intruder, I continued on my way. When I reached the first floor, I could hear the faint sound of gunfire that I guessed must be coming from Sam's computer. Continuing up the next flight of stairs I was faced with a small landing and a closed door. It was painted a deep shade of red that contrasted vividly with the green walls surrounding it.

As I made my way along the stretch of bare and worn floorboards leading to his bedroom, a loose board creaked loudly under the weight of my body as I stood on it. Instantly, the gunfire noise stopped and the air was filled with silence.

All I could hear was the steady beating of my heart as I walked slowly towards the attic door, unsure of what I would find on the other side. Just as I reached it and lifted my hand to knock, it swung abruptly open. And standing in front of me, dressed in the faded blue jeans and dark green T-shirt that he had worn to school that day was Sam, his face an unsmiling mask as he stared back at me. For some reason though, he did not seem at all surprised to see me and I had a strange feeling he already knew that I'd come to visit.

Swinging open the door, he turned around and headed back into his room without saying a word. Unsure what else to do, I followed along behind him.

Time for truth...

Sam sat silently on his bed, leaving the chair in front of his computer desk for me to sit on. He had exited the game he'd been playing and the screen was blank. The bright green lights of the power switch blinked at me as I sat down.

He did not say a word and was obviously waiting for me to speak. Breaking the uncomfortable silence, I opened my mouth intending to ask him how he was, or some other regular type of question. But instead, different words poured from my lips and I was powerless to stop them.

"Sam, tell me the truth. Can you really move things with

your mind or was what I saw yesterday some type of magic act?"

I could feel my face blushing a deep shade of red as I sat there awkwardly, waiting for his reply. I barely dared to breathe as I waited for an answer. The seconds seemed to tick by and I was ready to demand a response when the words finally came. Although they were not what I was expecting.

"What if I told you I was practicing for a magic show?" he stared at me solemn-faced, his mouth a determined line.

"I wouldn't believe you!" I replied, immediately jumping to my feet.

"Sam, come on, please tell me the truth. I promise you can trust me. I haven't told anyone what I saw. And I promise I never will, but I want to know what's going on."

His expression turned to one of surprise. "You haven't told anybody? Jake or the other kids at school? No one knows?"

"I swear I haven't told a soul!" I replied adamantly, watching his expression change once more. The relief was clear on his face as he stared back at me, but still, he wasn't ready to open up.

"I saw everything yesterday, Sam," I continued. "I know it wasn't magic. You were moving those things with your mind, weren't you? Please tell me." I repeated the words once more, my insistent tone willing him to tell me the truth.

Then, the unexpected happened. As if by magic, a pen that had been lying idle on the desk, was suddenly hovering in mid-air right in front of me.

I stared at it for a moment and by impulse, reached to grab it, but was not quick enough. Looking on in amazement, I watched it zip out of reach and fly across the room.

"Oh my gosh! It *is* true! You really *are* telekinetic!" I stared at Sam in astonishment, keeping one eye on him and one on the pen.

But at the mention of the word telekinetic, he turned quickly back towards me, a surprised expression on his face. And the pen fell to the floor.

"I googled it," I explained in a rush as I glanced at the fallen pen. "I know all about telekinesis. I also know that most scientists think it doesn't exist, that it's all done using tricks people aren't aware of."

His mouth turned up at the corners in a small grin and I could see that he was impressed. I'd done my homework and knew all about the crazy, incredible thing that he was able to do. Added to that, I wasn't calling him a freak or running from the room in terror. He knew I was genuinely interested. But for me, it was much more than that. I was in total awe and wanted to see more.

Jumping to my feet once again, I squealed. "Show me what else you can do!"

This was the most amazing thing I had ever seen or heard of. And it was happening right in front of my very eyes. I was filled to the brim with excitement and wanted to know everything.

Within seconds, there were items floating everywhere. A box of cut out foam shapes that had been shoved into a corner abruptly opened up and the pieces lifted into the air. Each time I tried to grab hold of one, it zipped away out of reach. It was incredible to see what he was capable of.

Obviously pleased with my reaction, he began to show off, and heavier items started to float around the room. A math textbook lifted up towards the ceiling and hovered there. Then it lowered to a spot right in front of me and I watched as one by one, each of the pages turned. Just as I reached to grasp hold of the book, the chair I was sitting on wheeled away towards the opposite wall where it was pinned in place. Try as I might, I could not budge it. And I giggled in response. That was when I became aware of the weirdest sensation.

My hair began to blow across my face and fly up into the air as though a rush of wind had whipped through the room and taken hold of it. I tried to smooth it down but it blew crazily around my head and face. I struggled to see, but when I did manage to brush the hair from my eyes, I realized nothing else in the room was moving and there was not even the slightest breath of a breeze coming from the open window.

Sam was causing the movement of every strand of hair. He sat deep in concentration as his mind created every single individual flick. When my hair finally settled and I was able to smooth it back into place, I stared at him in awe.

An endless list of questions raced through my head, ones that I was desperate to know the answers to. I wanted Sam to explain, to tell me how and why it was all possible. I was utterly fascinated and wanted to hear every single detail.

Then I remembered the incidents surrounding Jake. Caught up in my excitement, I'd momentarily forgotten my fears about Sam and the events I'd already witnessed. I was convinced that he was to blame for all the things that had happened, but could not bring myself to believe he'd intended to harm Jake.

Before I could say a word, we heard the sound of his mother's voice from the bottom of the stairs. "Sam? Tess? Are you guys coming down for cake? It's much nicer when it's straight from the oven!"
Sam looked at me and grinned. "I hope you like banana cake!"

Pushing all thoughts of Jake aside, I stared back at him and smiled. And for the first time, I was aware of a whole new sensation taking hold. It was kind of a rippling tingle working its way through my body as I took in the sight of his wide smile and shining brown eyes. I had never before seen his face light up that way. It was as though a transformation had taken place and a whole new person was sitting there in front of me. In that moment, I knew he couldn't hurt anyone. I was sure of it.

I recognized instantly that he was special. Not just because of his powers. There was more, a lot more to Sam Worthington than I had ever suspected. And with the shiver of excitement working its way right down to the tips of my toes, I stood up from my seat to follow him out of his bedroom and down the winding staircase.

There were many questions I wanted to be answered, but I was forced to be patient. Somehow though, I knew those answers would come. I was also convinced it was more than pure chance that I happened to move into the house next door. I believed in destiny and I was quite sure that I'd been destined to become a part of Sam's unique world.

With a silent prayer of thanks, I followed him down the spiral stairway, the delicious smell of a freshly baked banana and walnut cake becoming stronger with every step.

Excitement...

When I eventually fell into bed that night, my head was spinning with images of various shaped items floating in the air around me. The scene in Sam's bedroom as I sat utterly transfixed in the chair, played on my mind and I was far too excited to sleep.

My curtains were open and I stared out at the night sky, deep in thought. Right next door was a boy my age who could actually move things with his mind! All the kids at school thought he was weird, a loser and a loner and wanted nothing to do with him. But no one knew the real Sam. The boy who was actually a really nice person once you got to know him, and they certainly had no idea of what he was capable of. No one knew any of this. Except for his mom, of course. And now me.

The tingle of excitement that had taken a firm hold was still sitting in my stomach, bubbling and churning but I did not mind in the slightest. The grin on my face had remained fixed in place all afternoon and even my mother had commented on how happy I looked when I finally returned from Sam's house
.

"It seems that you and Sam are getting along well," she commented curiously.

"He and Mrs. Worthington are both really nice. We should have them over for dinner sometime." I replied in a matter of fact way as if it were no big deal.

I certainly did not want Mom taking my sudden interest in

Sam the wrong way. After all, we were just friends. And even though I reminded myself of that fact, I still could not help the tingle of excitement that erupted inside me, each time I thought of his smiling face.

But my mother was keen on the idea of inviting them over and approved of me being "neighborly" as she called it. If only she knew that our neighbors really were psychic and had powers beyond anything we could possibly imagine. The whole idea was so thrilling, I felt as though I were in the middle of a science fiction movie, and at any moment the director would say...That's a wrap! Or whatever it was that directors said when the filming of a movie was complete.

While the scene I'd just become involved with was actually real life, it was also far from over. In fact, for me, it had only just begun and I wondered excitedly what was in store next. At the sound of a sudden torrential downpour of rain, I jumped up to close my bedroom window. A loud crack of thunder boomed overhead and I scrambled quickly back to bed and under the covers. Snuggling deeper, I reveled in the distinct sound of heavy rain on the tin surface of our roof. The noise was almost deafening but at the same time I found it comforting and closed my eyes, sighing happily.

The next day could not come quickly enough and I could hardly wait for it to begin.

A day of surprises…

As it turned out, the next day did not go ahead as I'd imagined. I stood at the bus stop waiting impatiently for Sam to join me. We'd agreed to meet there and catch the bus to school together. But when the bus slowed to a halt and the doors swung open, I was forced to climb the steps on my own.

The bus pulled away from the curb and I stared out the window, willing Sam to suddenly appear before the bus gathered speed and disappeared down the road. That didn't happen though. There was no sign of him anywhere.

Making my way down the aisle, I found a seat to myself. I had decided that perhaps he'd slept in and would need to ask his mom for a lift. Hoping that was the case, I glanced out the window and watched the houses rush by in a blur. All I wanted was to get to school as quickly as possible so I could see him again.

When I joined my friends who were milling together in the usual spot, I could barely concentrate on anything they were saying. Instead, my focus was on the school entrance gate, waiting for the sight of Sam's familiar figure on the pavement in front of me. However, when the bell signaled the start of the school day and everyone had turned in the direction of their classrooms, he was still nowhere to be seen.

Disappointed and a little concerned, I made my way with the others towards our room, where I sat down in my seat at the back alongside a girl in our group called Tahlia Davis.

Struggling to concentrate on the work the teacher had directed us to complete, I kept one eye on the classroom door, hoping that Sam would suddenly arrive.

But when the bell rang for recess, I resigned myself to the fact that something unexpected must have forced him to stay away. I wondered if he'd become ill overnight and as I headed down the hallway with the other kids, further possibilities came to mind. Perhaps his mother was unwell and he'd been forced to stay at home to care for her. Or, worst case scenario, maybe one of them had been involved in an accident of some sort.

A wild assortment of ideas raced through my head but there was no way of knowing for sure what the real reason was. I would have to wait for the afternoon when I planned to go straight to his house to find out. I just hoped that nothing serious had happened.

Meanwhile, the main focus for everyone at school was the disco that was scheduled for the following week. As it was the only disco for the entire year, everyone was super excited and it was all they were interested in talking about.

I soon learned that Samantha Evans had agreed to go with a really cute boy in our class named Josh Hartley. They'd recently started going out together and the disco was their first official 'date'. It was the only thing Samantha could think about and she spent the entire recess laughing with the other girls who also had 'dates' for the disco.

Several of the girls, including Tahlia, were going out with boys in our grade, and it appeared that I was one of the few who wasn't.

This was something I wasn't used to. At my old school, the kids just hung out together and didn't really have girlfriends or boyfriends. Although my best friend, Casey, had a huge crush on a boy named Tom Jackson, it was just a secret crush and never eventuated into anything else. Apart from telling me, she kept this information secret. She would have died of embarrassment if anyone ever found out, especially Tom, himself. For her, that would have been the end of the world.

It seemed that things were very different at my new school though. In particular, amongst the group I'd become friendly with. Most of them had paired up with someone and it seemed the normal thing to do. I realized that among that group, I was the odd one out. Although Tahlia did warn me that Jake Collins was planning to ask me to go to the disco with him. This was something I found surprising. He was so popular, I thought he'd already have a girlfriend. Regardless of that though, going to the disco with Jake was not something I was interested in doing at all.

After being warned by Tahlia, I decided to spend the day trying to avoid him. I didn't know what I'd do if he did ask me. There was no way I'd say yes. But then if I said no, that would just be awkward.

Surrounded by talk of the disco, I had no choice but to join in with the chatter as everyone discussed the clothes they planned to wear. Tahlia had already been shopping and had an entirely new outfit organized. I listened enviously as she described the gorgeous skirt and top that her mom had bought for her at a local designer store in town.

All the while, I thought about the choices in my own cupboard at home and wondered if I could convince my mom to take me shopping for something new as well. If not, I guessed I'd have to make do with what I already owned. Although those choices were nowhere near as pretty as what the girls at school were describing.

But then I thought of Sam. And for the first time wondered if he would even be planning to go to the disco at all. I wasn't sure if it was something he'd even be interested in. If not, I knew I'd have to convince him because I really wanted him to go.

I also decided I'd invite him to hang out with me and the others when he was back at school, rather than keeping to himself. At the same time though, I knew he wouldn't fit in. It also occurred to me that perhaps I didn't really fit in either.

As it so happened though, my plans to hang out with Sam did not work out in the way I thought they would.

In fact, the afternoon's events took a very different path, one that I had certainly not expected.

Unexpected...

When I knocked on Sam's front door that afternoon, I thought his mom would greet me, once again her smiling face instantly making me welcome. But quite unexpectedly, there was no answer, and I was left to stand on the front doorstep surrounded by silence.

Trying again with a louder and more insistent knock, left me with the same result. No response. All I could hear was the rustle of the nearby trees in the gentle breeze, and nothing else.

Turning away with disappointment, there was nothing for me to do but return home. The mystery of Sam's absence at school that day remained exactly that, a mystery as yet unsolved. I had no idea what his phone number was and he didn't own a mobile, so I had no way of contacting him. I would just have to wait for his return.

Just as I neared the bushy border that edged the garden, I had the oddest sensation I was being watched. I could feel the hairs on my arms stand slightly on end and I glanced nervously behind me. The house really did have a spooky feel and if I didn't know better, I'd probably end up being one of the many who thought it haunted.

But there was no one in sight. I took a deep breath and convinced myself that it was probably just the whisper of the wind that was putting me on edge. That and the lonely feel of a run-down and neglected old house that appeared abandoned.

Then I spotted what I thought was an abrupt movement at the upstairs attic window, the room that Sam used as a bedroom. I walked back towards the house to take a closer look. Peering curiously upwards, I shaded my eyes from the bright rays of afternoon sunlight that were blurring my vision and preventing a clear view.

"Sam!" I called out loudly. "Sam, is that you?" I stood quietly waiting for someone to answer.

Deciding to give it one more try, I called out again. "Sam, if you're home, I'd really like to talk to you."

All I could see was the sheer fabric of the white curtain hanging from his open window above. It was being blown about by the breeze and from where I stood, it did seem to create a moving shape. I decided that it must have been the curtain that had caught my eye.

Keen to move away from the uncomfortable silence and the eerie sensations that were affecting my senses, I turned back towards the garden and hurried across the stretch of open grass. When I reached the tree line and was about to step onto the overgrown track that led to my house, I heard a voice calling my name.

Whipping my head around in surprise, I spotted Sam at the front door beckoning for me to come inside. So I headed back to the house once again.

"I didn't think anyone was home!" I exclaimed, confused at his sudden appearance. "I called out to you but there was no answer!"

I followed him inside and waited for an explanation. I was sure it had been him watching me from his room, and I wondered why he was behaving so strangely.

"Is your mom at home?" I asked curiously, beginning to feel a little uncomfortable.

My stomach was churning uneasily, the odd expression on his face was unreadable and I wasn't sure what was going on. Although I could sense that something was definitely wrong.

Shaking his head to indicate that his mother was not at home, he finally chose to speak. "No, she's out. I'm not sure what time she'll be back."

I stared at him then, waiting for him to continue. At the same time, I glanced around the house and noticed some broken items in a pile on the living room floor. What looked like a shattered vase and a couple of other broken bits and pieces were lying in a heap. They'd obviously been swept together but were yet to be cleared away.

"Why weren't you at school today?" I asked the question mainly to break the uncomfortable silence, rather than to get the answer that I'd been waiting all day to hear.
Sighing heavily, he looked at me and shook his head but did not say a word. Instead, he turned around and walked slowly towards the kitchen, indicating for me to follow him. I had no idea what was going on or why he was behaving so strangely. But there was something in his manner that made me more curious than ever. When I reached the kitchen, I found him seated on a tall stool, staring blankly my way.

I looked questioningly at him, waiting for him to speak. I had so many questions and didn't know where to begin. I wasn't sure if he really wanted me there, but he'd invited me in and I was determined to finally get some answers. Perching myself on a stool alongside him, I sat down quietly and gave him a small smile of encouragement, hoping that he might choose to open up after all.

Perhaps he sensed my mood and knew what I was waiting for. I really wasn't sure. But a moment later, he began to talk. And once he started, he did not stop. It was as though a dam had burst and was finally given the freedom to flow. I had the feeling that he'd been waiting for exactly that…someone who was simply willing to sit and listen.

And as I sat silently, my mouth slightly agape at what I was hearing, he shared his entire incredible story. Right from the beginning, he told me everything. And I think I can remember just about every single detail.

Sam's story...

"I had no idea I could move things without touching them. I thought I was a regular kid, just like everyone else. But then one day, just after my 6th birthday, Mom and I were at the shopping center and I saw a man standing at the front of a toy store demonstrating a remote control spaceship. It had flashing lights and made all kinds of sounds as it lifted into the air. I thought it was the coolest thing I'd ever seen.

I remember running into the store and grabbing one off the shelf. I'd spotted them on display and I insisted that Mom buy one for me. But my dad had just left us. It was only a few days before this that he went out to buy a loaf of bread and never came back!

Anyway, money was really tight. So Mom said no.

I don't know why I behaved the way I did. Maybe it was because my dad had taken off and I was acting out. But I remember it all so clearly, it could have happened yesterday.

When Mom refused to buy it for me, I freaked out. And I mean, I really freaked out! She wouldn't listen to me. But I wanted her to listen. I had to have that toy and all she could say was, "No, we can't afford it!"

I could feel my body heating up and this intense pressure beginning to form in my head. I kept asking and asking and she kept saying no. She tried to drag me out of there but I refused to budge. It was like my feet were glued to the floor.

All of a sudden, the pressure got worse and I thought my head was going to explode. Then, out of the blue, the overhead lights started to flicker on and off, on and off. It was the weirdest thing. At the time, I had no idea I was causing it. The only thing I was aware of was the pounding in my brain; as well as the fact that I had to have that toy. I was still holding the box in my hands and wouldn't let it go.

That was when toys and boxes and packets of all different shapes and sizes started falling off the shelves around us. I remember the shocked look on my mom's face. She was asking if I was okay but all I could do was stare. And the whole time, the throbbing in my head was getting worse and worse.

Then everything went black.

The next thing I remember is my mom shaking me and yelling at me to stop.
Nothing like that has ever happened again. Well, not in public anyway…except for maybe once or twice just recently that is."

Sam glanced at me then, the guilt obvious on his face. I was certain he was referring to the 'Jake incidents'. But I didn't comment. I just let him continue.

"Later on Mom asked me what happened. I told her I didn't know. She gave me the strangest look but never mentioned it again. That was until my 9th birthday. That was the next major event and when we both knew for sure that I possessed some type of power.

We were planning a family celebration that night. If you can call me, my mom and her boyfriend, a family that is. During the afternoon, Mom took me to the park. But we made it home just in time for my favorite TV show. It was a cartoon series, all about these people who lived in a futuristic space age. I loved it. I thought it was the best show ever and I watched it every afternoon.

That day, Ron, my mom's boyfriend, came home early from work. This never happened. He never came home early. Except for that day. As soon as he walked in, he grabbed a beer from the fridge, sat down in our comfiest chair and changed the TV channel. He didn't even ask me, and it was right in the middle of the most exciting part of my favorite show.

Right from the start, I'd never liked him. He had a real mean streak and was always yelling at me. 'Sam, go get me a drink. Sam pick up your stuff. Sam go and help your mother.'

He wasn't even my dad and thought he could boss me around all the time. I hated it.

He had no right to change the channel without even asking

me. So I told him to switch it back. He had the TV remote control, otherwise, I would have done it myself.

I mean, it was my birthday and all. I just wanted to watch my favorite TV show. Surely that was fair enough.

But he told me to be quiet and stop whining or he'd send me to my room. I was so sick of him bossing me around. It was the last straw.

I clearly remember focusing on the beer bottle in his hand. He was sitting there ignoring me and laughing at some stupid commercial. But all I could see was that beer bottle. I don't think I was aware of what I was doing. I was just angry and the more I stared at him, the angrier I became.

Then, without any warning, the bottle exploded in his hands. He was soaked with beer. It was all over him and he jumped out of his seat like a bomb had exploded in his lap. It was the funniest thing I'd ever seen in my life.

Because I was laughing so hard, he got angry with me and made me clean it up. But I didn't care. It was worth it. He even cut his hand and had to get bandages. He so deserved it though."

Sam chuckled at the memory and I looked on in silence, picturing the scene in my mind. I also wondered how I would have felt if it had been me in his place. I was sure that I would have been just as angry.
Taking a deep breath, he continued.

"Ron had no idea that I was to blame. But somehow I knew I was responsible. I could feel it inside. It was the strangest sensation and I don't know why it all came to me that day. Mom had never talked about the toy shop incident and I'd pretty much forgotten about it. But that afternoon, it all came back and that was when I realized.

I was happy to go to my room. Anything to get away from Ron. And besides that, I had stuff to figure out. I can see myself now. I was sitting on the floor just looking at the things in my room. Then I spotted an empty glass on a shelf next to my bed, and without even planning it, I started concentrating on the glass. At first, nothing happened, there was no movement at all and I wondered if the broken beer bottle was an accident and had nothing to do with me after all.

But then the glass moved. It was only a tiny vibration at first, so small that I barely noticed it. Then, the more I concentrated, the more the glass shook. Until eventually it fell onto its side.

I was really excited! It was so cool! I'd made something move with my mind. It was the most exciting thing I'd ever done. I can still remember how happy I was. It was the best birthday present ever!

Before I knew it, I had that glass hovering in mid-air. I laughed so much that I lost concentration and it smashed onto the floor.

That was when I heard Ron yelling at my mom. He sometimes did that and I had no idea why she put up with it.

But it was my birthday and I'd just made the biggest discovery of my life. So I ignored them and tried to focus on something else. All I could hear though was Ron's voice. By that stage, he sounded really angry and I guessed that something must've upset him and my mom was copping it.

I couldn't stand it any longer and I ran out to the kitchen. I'd had enough of Ron. I was sick of his yelling. I hated the way he treated my mom and I hated the way he treated me. And as well, it was my birthday and he was ruining it.

I told him to stop. I told him to leave my mom alone.

But he pushed me aside and I fell against one of the cupboards. That just made me angrier than ever.

It was like I was back in the toy shop all over again, but this time, it was much worse. A really intense burning sensation filled my head. I thought I was on fire from the inside. It just seemed to get hotter and hotter. And then without warning, everything went black.

I think I was only out for a few seconds but when I opened my eyes again, Ron was pinned against the wall. One minute he'd been standing right in front of me and the next, it was as though he'd been propelled across the kitchen.

That was when he knew. He knew that somehow I'd done it. I had caused that to happen. Mom knew as well. I could see it in her eyes. But I didn't care. I'd had enough.

It must've really scared him though because he grabbed his stuff and took off. Just like my dad, he disappeared and we never heard from him again.

Until last night that is. He turned up in the middle of the night knocking on our door. Can you believe it? He thinks that after all this time, he can just come walking back into our lives.

"Oh my gosh!" I exclaimed, "Your mom's boyfriend came back?"

Sam nodded his head and I watched as his jaw clenched with anger.

"Yeah, out of the blue he just turned up. He walked inside as if he owned the place. And then he asked my mom for money. When she said she didn't have any to give him, he started pushing her around. I got so angry. I knew I couldn't let him stay. I couldn't let it happen all over again."

I waited quietly for him to continue, all the while imagining how scary it must have been.

"I had to get rid of him somehow. So I started using my mind power to pick things up and throw them at him. Stuff was flying at him from all directions. I broke Mom's favorite vase. I didn't mean to do it but I had to get rid of him. I couldn't let him come back."

I sat frozen in my seat, finding it difficult to comprehend that something so terrible had been happening while at the same time I was curled up in bed, sound asleep and oblivious to what was going on.

"He got the message though." Sam continued with a grin. "You should have seen the look on his face. He was so freaked out, he took off out the front door and disappeared. I broke a heap of mom's stuff but it was worth it to see him run off like a scared chicken. I just hope he doesn't come back!"

I stared at Sam, my mouth still slightly agape as I pictured the scene he'd just described. Speechless and unsure what to say, I sat quietly, totally overwhelmed by it all.

Sitting in silence alongside him, I tried to imagine what he'd been through. It was clearly the reason he hadn't gone to school that day. And I could hardly blame him. How could he even think about school after an experience such as that?

I realized right then, how different his life was to my own. It was so hard to even try to comprehend. With no idea how to respond and unable to look him in the eye, I focused on the floorboards at my feet; my heart overflowing with sympathy for the mysterious boy sitting beside me.

Then, from the corner of my eye, I risked a glance and watched as he flicked away the loose strands of hair that insisted on falling into his eyes. Those intense brown eyes that were like dark pools of silk, catching the last rays of sunlight as it shone through the kitchen window.

I had so many questions, but I knew they would have to wait. It was not the time to be bombarding him with things I still wanted to know. And besides that, I'd promised my mom I'd be home to help with dinner.

So I left him alone, sitting on that tall stool at the kitchen bench; deep in thought with his memories haunting him.

But I took comfort in the smile he gave me when I told him I'd see myself out. And more than that, it was his words that gave me hope; a hope that in some small way, I'd managed to help him.

"Thanks for coming over, Tess. It feels good to talk to someone."

And with that I waved goodbye, inviting him over to my house whenever he felt like talking again.

I decided to leave him be. If he wanted to talk some more, he knew where I was. In the meantime, his secret would lay safe, buried deep inside away from prying eyes and evil gossip.

Knowing that he trusted me to keep his secret meant more than anything.

Unexpected...

It was three days later that I answered a knock at the door. We'd just finished eating dinner and after helping to tidy the kitchen, I was heading to my room to get some homework done. That was when I heard a gentle tapping and I tentatively opened the door, as we had not been expecting anyone and I had no idea who the person could possibly be.

Feeling my heart skip a beat, I stood staring at Sam, who looked back at me with an uncertain grin attached to his face. He hadn't been at school and I hadn't seen him since I last visited his house. Until that moment, I'd had no idea when I would see him again or how much time he planned to take off school. And when he hadn't shown up for the third day in a row, I was wondering if I would ever see him again. Then, out of the blue, there he was standing on my front doorstep.

"Hi!" he said shyly, his smile widening slightly.

"Hi!" I answered back, unable to help my own beaming smile. "It's good to see you."

"Thanks!" he responded, raising his eyebrows slightly. "Good to see you too."
I stood there a little awkwardly caught up in the silence between us. It seemed as though neither of us knew what to say to the other.

Abruptly, I realized he was waiting to be invited inside. Feeling a little silly, I opened the door wide, "Do you want to come in?"

"Ah, yeah," he chuckled with a slight nod of his head. "That'd be good."

Following me through to the living room, he greeted my parents who were both in their favorite recliner chairs in front of the television.

I stood alongside Sam while he chatted politely. He answered all my mom's questions about school and his own mother, as well as her curiosity surrounding what his mom did for a job. She even suggested the idea of asking Sam's mom to do a psychic reading for her sometime.

I rolled my eyes when I heard her say that. I knew she was just being polite. She was so conservative when it came to that sort of thing and did not believe in psychics at all. In my mother's opinion, if something could not be proved by science, then it must be fake. Well, if only she knew!

Instead, she was oblivious to the fact that Sam was living proof this theory was all wrong. The skills he was capable of had been disproved by scientists over and over but just like my mom, these scientists were unaware that telekinesis was real.

I knew it, Sam knew it. But I was one hundred percent certain that my mother would never believe it if I told her. Even if she saw Sam in action, she'd accuse him of using magic tricks. Just like all those scientists have done in the past.

As much as I loved science, I was learning that there were many more factors to take into consideration and also that we shouldn't simply rely on "science" alone for all our answers.

Eventually, Sam and I were able to move away from my mom's interrogation and make our way upstairs to my room. I explained to her that we'd be using the telescope, as the conditions were perfect for star gazing and looking at the night sky.

Luckily for us, it actually was a great night to be searching the galaxy. And usually, I would love the opportunity to be sharing this amazing hobby with someone else. But, there was something much more important that I wanted to talk to Sam about and finally, I had the opportunity.

But when we reached my room, Sam, who was unable to ignore the temptation, headed straight for the telescope and was immediately absorbed in the incredible view in front of him.

While he was busy adjusting the focus, I blurted out impulsively, "I've missed you at school. Are you planning on coming back?"

He looked at me in surprise, taken aback by my comment. I could see that he wasn't used to people speaking their mind. But if he was going to hang out with me, this was something he would have to get used to.

"Ah, yeah," he stammered, not quite sure how to respond. "I guess I'll be at school tomorrow."

"That's great!" I replied. "Miss Browne is doing a heap of revision for our tests next week, so it's probably a good idea."

He returned his attention to the telescope, which was

obviously something he was keen to take advantage of while he had the chance. Unable to focus on astronomy right then, I continued on.

"Are you going on the field trip next week?" I asked curiously. "It should be really cool. Everyone says that the science center in town is amazing."
"I don't know," he replied, as he kept his gaze on the telescope eyepiece, turning it in a different direction.

"I'm not really keen on field trips," he added briefly.

"You have to go!" I responded. "Have you ever been there before? It'll be such a great day. You really shouldn't miss it. And apparently, there's a planetarium there. It will be so cool!"

I realized I was babbling on, but I felt a little nervous. I was still overwhelmed by what he'd shared with me only a few days earlier. Although I didn't want to mention any of that, and it seemed that he didn't either.

I had hardly stopped thinking about it though. Sam and his story had been on my mind ever since. I'd been thinking about other things as well; the questions that I was desperate to finally hear the answers to. So far I hadn't worked up the courage, but I wanted to know the answers once and for all.

I stood watching him as he stared into the telescope, totally absorbed in the night sky that was displaying its beautiful glory, and my mind ticked over. I knew I should just say what I wanted to say. I usually had no trouble with that sort of thing, but this time, it seemed different. I guess I'd never had to tackle such a sensitive issue before. And now that he'd told me about his past, I guessed he had good reason to behave the way he did. Regardless though, I still couldn't accept it. I had to know the truth.

Taking a deep breath, I decided to take the plunge.

"It was you who caused all those accidents for Jake, wasn't it? The broken glass of milk in the canteen? The tray of food that he 'accidentally' spilled all over himself? The locker door suddenly flying open and the broom landing on his head? That was all you, wasn't it, Sam?"

He kept his focus on the telescope and his gaze on the eyepiece, but I saw his body stiffen. Although he did not say a word. He didn't turn to look at me either.

Sighing deeply, I refused to stop there. "And what about the football that somehow connected with Jake's head that day, when we were all outside for lunch break?"

There was still no response from Sam. And no further reaction.

"What about the tree branch, Sam? Was that you? Was it you who caused that?"

He spun around and looked at me, fear in his eyes. But he didn't speak. I could read his expression though, and I was sure he was worried about how I would react; now that I knew the whole truth.

And so he should be concerned. While I was now aware of what he'd been through over the years, it didn't excuse him. The incidents with Jake weren't minor. Especially the tree branch. And when I thought about the near miss that day, I felt an anger well inside me.

"Sam! If that branch had hit Jake, he could've been badly

hurt, maybe even killed!"

My breathing had quickened and I felt my heart racing. "I know Jake can be mean sometimes but what you did was serious. He didn't deserve that!"

At the mention of Jake's name, Sam was the one to react. I saw the irritation flare in his eyes as he glared at me. "He didn't deserve it? Are you kidding me?"

As he moved away from the telescope, I could see his fists clench at the mere mention of Jake's name.

"All he does is bully other kids. Haven't you seen it? Or are you too blind, just like all the other girls at school? He's the meanest kid there is and all he does is put everyone down, just to make himself feel better!"

I backed away from him then. He seemed to have suddenly worked himself into a rage and I was frightened about what he'd do next.

As if in answer to my fear, I watched him focus on the chair by my side. Then, without warning, and as if by magic, it scraped rapidly across the floorboards, dragging the throw rug as it went. It was as though it had been flung to the other side of the room, where it hit the wall with a loud bang and then toppled over.

Gasping in shock, I stood silently in my spot, not daring to say a word. There was no way I wanted to risk upsetting him further. Then I heard my mother's footsteps in the hallway and turned to find her standing in the doorway.

"What was that noise?" she asked, her brows knitted together in a concerned frown.

Gulping, I glanced at the fallen chair and the crumpled rug. She followed my gaze and then looked from me to Sam, her frown furrowing deeper.

She hesitated for a moment as she took in the scene in front of her. And then she spoke, her annoyed tone indicating a command, not a question. "Don't you have homework you need to finish, Tess?"

She looked at Sam then, the frown still in place on her brow, "It's getting late, Sam. It's probably time you went home."

I could see that she was not at all impressed. I also knew that there'd be questions later on. Questions I did not think I'd be able to answer.

Glancing apologetically at me, Sam made his way to the door, edging past my mother.

"Goodbye, Mrs. Hawkins. Thanks for having me." He mumbled the words, in an attempt to be polite.

But the air was thick with awkward tension as I followed him down the stairs and opened the front door.

"Bye Sam," I whispered quietly, as he made his way down the front steps.

Before he disappeared into the darkness, I called out softly, "Will I see you at school tomorrow?"

He murmured a response that I didn't catch and all I could do was stand at the door and watch him vanish into the night.

For some reason, I was ridden with guilt and blamed myself for his reaction. I wondered if perhaps, after all, he really did have good reason to behave the way he had; especially concerning Jake.

Regardless of what Jake had done though, Sam's behavior had been dangerous. And I was beginning to understand the depth of what he was capable of.

Making my way past the living room, I avoided my mother's annoyed expression and headed quietly up the stairs to my room, closing the door behind me.

When I put the chair back in its place in front of my computer desk and straightened the crumpled rug, I sat down and picked up a pen in an attempt to get some homework done. But try as I might, I could not concentrate on school work.

Instead, it was Sam's face that remained foremost in my mind.

The standoff...

Sam did not show up at school for the remainder of the week. I was quite sure his visit to my house had caused him to stay away. Clearly, my comments about Jake had upset him and I felt very guilty about that. But on the other hand, I was still concerned by Sam's reaction. I was also worried by what he might be capable of doing should he ever really lose control.

That didn't stop me from wanting to see him though. The more I thought about everything he'd shared with me, the more I sympathized with his behavior. I decided I had no right to judge him and when I remembered the way I felt when he was around me, I felt more confused than ever.

He remained constantly in my thoughts. When I was at home in my room, I kept listening out for the sound of his voice from beyond the garden. There were a few times when I heard his mother calling to him, but apart from that there was only silence and I never once heard Sam at all.

Regardless, I walked out my front door each day hoping to see his familiar figure waiting at the bus stop across the road. But this never happened. It was then a huge surprise to see him step out from his mom's car after it pulled up at the school gate one morning the following week. I was so used to him being away that his sudden appearance at school was totally unexpected. From where I stood, hidden from sight by the group of kids I was standing amongst, I watched as she waved goodbye and sped off down the road.

Sam made his way through the gate, eyes downcast as usual. It took all the restraint I could muster not to call out or rush over to greet him. I knew he'd hate attracting attention and the last thing I wanted was to embarrass him. It seemed though, I wasn't the only one to notice his arrival. Within seconds Jake Collins had also spotted him and decided to make sure everyone else knew as well.

"Hey, loser! You're back! We've missed you, buddy. Where have you been?" Jake's loud voice carried across the tops of all the others and instantly, just about every head turned in response.

I cringed at the sound of Jake's laughter, as well as the way he glanced around to make sure everyone was watching. Meanwhile, Sam continued along the pavement without acknowledging Jake at all. But Jake was not impressed by this. He was after a reaction and I knew he would not let it go.

"Hey! You didn't answer my question! Don't you know it's rude not to answer when people speak to you?"

Jake moved onto the walkway, blocking Sam's path. And all Sam could do was attempt to step around him. This amused Jake even more and with a wide smirk, he side-stepped in front of Sam, once again blocking his way.

From the spot where I was standing, I had a clear view, and I became more anxious as the seconds ticked by. I was sure Sam would react and this would cause more trouble. But surprisingly enough, he didn't respond at all. Instead, he continued to ignore Jake. Though this was not the reaction Jake wanted.

"Hey, are you deaf or something? Psycho freak!" It seemed the last two words were added as an afterthought and Jake glared angrily down at the boy in front of him.

It was then that Sam stopped dead in his tracks and glared back. His eyes had become dark with anger but still, he did not say a word. How he managed to stay silent was beyond me. I was sure that if I were in his situation, I, myself would find it hard to stay in control.

Worried that he may actually be ready to explode, I raced over to try and prevent what could become a disaster.

"Jake!" I frowned crossly at him. "Why don't you just leave Sam alone?"

I didn't want to create a scene. But I could not stand by any longer. With my heart thumping wildly, I peered anxiously at Jake.

Turning towards the sound of my voice, he stared at me in surprise. Then with an evil smirk, he looked back at Sam. "So you need a girl to stick up for you, hey? What a loser!"

Giving Sam another shove, he turned away and sauntered off. And when he reached his friends, who stood nearby watching the scene unfold, he looked around with a smug grin.

All I could do was stare back in disgust, at the same time, realizing Sam had every right to be angry. That morning, I finally saw Jake for what he really was and wondered why I hadn't seen it before. But right then I could do nothing except watch Sam continue quickly towards the steps leading into the school building and disappear out of sight.

Understanding…

From my seat at the back of the room, I tried to concentrate on the Math lesson that Miss Browne was teaching. But I barely took in a word. The entire time, my thoughts were on the incident I'd witnessed that morning. That as well as Sam himself, and I could not help but continually glance towards him as he sat in his seat on the other side of the room. He seemed absorbed in the lesson and kept his gaze focused on either our teacher or the Math book on his desk.

When Miss Browne asked us to choose a partner to complete an activity involving the use of dice and a series of Math operations, finally I caught him looking my way. Instantly our eyes connected and it was clear that each of us had the same thought. Just as I stood to head across the room towards his desk, Tahlia Johnson grabbed my arm and pulled me back.

"Tess, where are you going?" she asked curiously.

I could feel the dismay in my stomach as I glanced apologetically at Sam. Tahlia expected me to be her partner. She sat alongside me and we'd become used to being partners for everything. I knew she expected this occasion to be no different to any other. So I had no option but to sit back down and join her.

Watching from my spot, I saw Sam resign himself to the idea of working with Jasmine, the smartest girl in the class and the girl who sat next to him. For the remainder of the lesson, I was unable to focus at all. Tahlia became frustrated because I kept making mistakes by putting numbers in the wrong places. In the end, I gave up and let her finish the activity on her own. She was aiming for a perfect score and was more than happy to take over. Luckily she was good at Math and didn't really need my help. Although she was unimpressed that Jasmine and Sam had finished before her and scored 100 percent.

Later on, when the bell rang for recess, I spotted Sam making his way quickly out the classroom door. He was gone from sight before I'd barely had a chance to leave my seat. But when I followed my friends towards the usual place where we sat during lunch breaks, I caught sight of him. He was sitting under his favorite tree, the place where I noticed he often sat, obviously because it was in an isolated spot away from kids like Jake. He was actually seated on the far side of the tree, with his face blocked from view. But a flash of the blue jeans and shirt he was wearing that day, happened to catch my eye.

Making a quick decision, I stood without warning and told Tahlia I'd be back later. Before she had a chance to protest or ask where I was going, I walked quickly towards the tree and plopped down on the grass alongside him.

"Hey!" I said, as I smiled in greeting, "Is it okay if I sit here?"

Sam glanced at me in surprise before nodding his head. "Aah, yeah sure! If you want to."

A wide smile still on my face, I offered him one of the chocolate chip cookies from my lunch box. "Would you like one? I can guarantee they won't be as good as your mom's home baking though!"

"Sure," he laughed, and I could sense him instantly relax as he took one of the cookies and bit hungrily into it.

"Actually, these are pretty good!" he grinned as I offered him another.

"Jake's a real jerk!" the words popped out of my mouth unexpectedly. I had not planned to make that comment and surprised not only Sam but myself as well.

Once the words had left my lips, I was forced to repeat them. And this time with even more conviction. "I admit it's taken me a while to see through him, but he really is a jerk!"

Sam stared at me for a moment before opening his mouth to respond. "Wow!" The look of surprise remained on his face. "So you've finally figured that out, huh?"

"Yes!" I replied, with a firm nod of my head. "And I'm sorry I judged you! I had no right, and I understand why you did what you did."

Sam stared at me once again, bewildered. "You really are full of surprises!"

"I still think the falling tree branch was a bit much though! I mean seriously, you could have killed him!"

I held my breath, waiting for his response. But I wanted to be sure he knew exactly how I felt about the situation. I just hoped he would see my point of view and realize exactly how dangerous that situation had been. Much to my relief though, he agreed.

"Yeah, I know!" he admitted guiltily, glancing towards the spot where the tree branch had fallen as if recalling the incident in his mind. "That was a big mistake. I've never done anything like that before. He just made me so angry, I couldn't help it. I know that's no excuse. But he went too far. I was sick of him treating me that way and I guess I lost control."

I sat quietly, taking in his words. Finally, I understood. I understood how Sam felt and I understood his actions. Although I still thought he'd over-reacted, I was able to see his point of view. And added to that, I was in total awe over the things he was capable of.

On impulse, I blurted out something I'd been thinking about for days. "I want you to teach me!"

"What?" he asked, with a curious grin. "What do you want me to teach you?"

"How to move things with my mind," I replied, smiling excitedly. "The way you do."

He shook his head, an amused expression on his face. "It's not that simple."

"Why not?" I asked, my voice filling with excitement. The more I considered the idea, the more adamant I became. "I've researched telekinesis on the internet and there's heaps of sites explaining how to do what you do."

He laughed some more before adding. "That stuff won't work! It's not something you can learn. It's something you're born with."

Not willing to accept no for an answer, I continued on, my tone more persuasive than ever, "I've read all about it and there's tons of instructions. There's even YouTube videos demonstrating how it's done. But surely I could learn much quicker if you taught me. I mean, after all, you're an expert!"

"I don't know," he shook his head once more, "I'm not sure it's possible. I really don't know if I could teach you."

Then, grinning widely and as if it were an afterthought, he added the words I was hoping to hear, "But I guess we could give it a try."

"Yes!" I squealed, delightedly. "Sam, thank you so much! You're the best!" And without even thinking about it, I threw my arms around his neck in a quick hug.

Ignoring his startled expression, I jumped to my feet. "This afternoon I'll come to your house and we can get started." I could feel my excitement mounting at the thought. "I've got to get back to the others now. But I'll talk to you later."

And with that, I ran off in the direction of Tahlia and the

other girls. But when I joined them, all I could think about was the afternoon ahead of me and the strange but wonderful boy who had become my friend.

Deep down inside, I knew that my life was about to change. But rather than fear the unknown, I welcomed it. And right then, I could hardly wait for the school day to end.

The lesson…

When I told my mom I'd arranged to hang out with Sam that afternoon, she was unhappy.

"I'm not sure you should be spending so much time with him, Tess. He seems nice enough but there's something odd about him. I just haven't been able to work out what it is yet."

I shook my head at her reaction. "Mom, Sam's great! You just have to give him a chance. And besides, all I'm doing is going over to his house. He just lives next door, you know."

She frowned at me then, unconvinced. Much to my surprise, she hadn't mentioned his previous visit and the sight of the fallen chair in my room. But I didn't want to risk a lecture right then, so before she could say another word, I raced out the door.

"I'll be back in time to help you with dinner." I flashed a quick smile in her direction before disappearing into the bushy border at the edge of our garden.

I'd been waiting all day for this moment and did not want to miss out. When I pushed my way through the undergrowth and stepped into the open space of Sam's backyard, I immediately spotted him at the front door. It was as though he knew I was on my way and was waiting patiently for me, a grin stuck to his handsome face.

As I made my way across the overgrown lawn, I took in his appearance. I could see that he'd changed his clothes since arriving home from school. Dressed in a white T-shirt, oversized and frayed at the edges, it hung low over his black skinny jeans, which I'd never seen him wear before. I wondered if they were new or if he just saved them for special occasions. I smiled to myself at that possibility and at the same time, admired how great he looked. The afternoon sun shone on the highlights in his dark hair which hung in long strands over one eye and I realized in that moment how good looking he really was.

Overcome with an uncharacteristic shyness, I smiled at him a little awkwardly, wishing I'd taken more time with my own appearance. I was still dressed in the outfit I'd worn to school that day, a fitted white T-shirt and a pair of blue denim overalls. They were an old favorite but I could definitely have changed into something nicer. He didn't seem to mind though and welcomed me inside, the smile still wide on his face.

With a tingle of nervous excitement, I followed him to the kitchen where he offered me some of his mom's never-ending home baking. This time, instead of banana cake, it was a cake made with carrots and raisins. To me, the combination sounded strange but the cake itself was topped with creamy white icing and it looked delicious.

When I bit into the first mouthful, I found it was every bit as good as it looked and I could not resist a second slice.

"OMG! Your mom makes the best cakes!" I licked the icing off my fingers and pushed my plate aside. "Please take that cake away, or I won't be able to stop!"

He laughed in response and I watched as the large platter, topped with the remaining cake, lifted gently into the air of its own accord. It then hovered in front of me just out of reach before zooming across the kitchen, towards the open door of the fridge. The door slammed shut with the cake intact inside.

I stared at Sam in amazement. "That's incredible! Seriously, I want to know how you do it. Please tell me everything!"

His face lit up with laughter, and I could see he was pleased with my reaction. Then, clearly showing off, he began to focus on other items around him. Pieces of fruit from the nearby fruit bowl hovered in the air, the kitchen door opened, and a knife and fork lifted up above the bench top, in a cutting motion, as if slicing into a piece of food.

Cupboard doors began opening and closing, as other bits and pieces zipped around in front of me. I watched in awe as bowls and plates and dishes floated gently by and then a second later, whipped past so quickly, I was forced to twist and turn my head in an attempt to take it all in.

Then, in the blink of an eye, it all came to a sudden halt and I stared in shock as everything crashed to the floor.

"Sam! What do you think you're doing?" Turning abruptly towards the sound of the angry voice behind me, I caught sight of his mother, her face a mixture of rage and distress.

Shaking her head in dismay, she glared at Sam, her eyes filled with fury. Gone was the friendly person who I'd taken such a liking to and in her place stood a woman extremely upset, to say the least, at the sight of the scenario she had unexpectedly encountered.

"I don't understand you, Sam!" His mom glanced from him to me, but Sam did not say a word.

I guessed it was pointless trying to explain. Anyone could see what he'd been up to. But it was also obvious that what he'd been doing was not allowed, especially in front of other people. And that he would probably face some serious consequences after I left.

I glanced sympathetically towards him, as I bent down and began to pick up the shattered pieces of crockery that littered the floor around my feet. I kept my eyes on the floor and didn't dare look his mom's way as she stormed from the room.

All I heard were her last words as she disappeared from sight. "Clean up the mess, Sam! And you'll be using your allowance money to replace everything that's broken!"

"There goes the new computer game I've been saving up for," he murmured quietly as he bent down to help me.

I was at a loss for what to say. Sam tried to ease the tension by reassuring me that his mom would be fine. "She tends to over-react," he laughed in an attempt at humor.

I raised my eyebrows at that comment. "It must run in the family," I muttered quietly to myself and then glanced at Sam, hoping he hadn't heard.

I was still slightly shaken and felt completely responsible. After all, if I hadn't insisted on coming over and being taught telekinesis in the first place, the incident would never have happened. It was clearly my fault and I was to blame. I decided right then that I'd contribute to the cost of replacing everything. It was certainly the least I could do.

After picking up what we could, Sam grabbed a broom and swept up the remaining mess. Before no time, the kitchen was once again in order and except for the large pile that topped the trash can, there was no evidence of any breakage.

"Let's go up to my room," Sam whispered quietly. "So we can continue our lesson."

He grinned mischievously and turned towards the stairs, taking them two at a time in his hurry to reach his private sanctuary as quickly as possible. I followed along behind, struggling to catch my breath as I tried to keep up with him. When I finally reached the landing at the top, I immediately spotted him through his open door. His back was towards me and he appeared to be standing stock still and staring straight ahead.

When I entered the room, I closed the door quietly behind me, not wanting his mother to overhear our conversation or appear at the doorway unannounced. Once was enough for one afternoon and as I watched him concentrating on the items hovering in the air around his head, I knew she'd be furious if she caught him at it again.

As well as that, I was ready to learn an incredible new skill, the skill of moving things with my mind. And I certainly did not want to be interrupted.

When I eventually climbed into bed later that night, my head was swimming with images of books, pens, pencils, cups, plates and cutlery items hovering in the air in front of me. Then with no warning whatsoever, as soon as I tried to grab hold of them they zoomed quickly out of reach.

I recalled every moment that I'd been with Sam, right from the minute I arrived on his doorstep and he was standing there to greet me. It had been a magical afternoon, one I will never forget and as I lay in bed, still too excited to even think about sleeping, I remembered every detail, every word that Sam had spoken.

"It takes intense focus," he had said, a serious tone in his voice. "It looks easy and for me it is easy. But that's only after years of practice."

I sat listening carefully and tried to mimic every action he took. But it was instantly clear that his power came from deep within and required avid and intense concentration.

"At first, I struggled," he explained to me. "Especially when I was hanging out in my room and trying to move things just for fun. I realized very early on that it was much easier when I was experiencing some type of inner emotion."

"Emotion?" I asked curiously. "What type of emotion?"

"Well, anger is definitely the most effective!"

I recalled his expression. Immediately, I'd comprehended

the meaning behind his words. I had already seen what anger had made him capable of but it helped me to understand what he was saying.

"Anger seems to give me the most power. When I'm angry, I don't even think about what I'm doing. It's like an automatic reaction, a response to the intensity of what I'm feeling inside."

I continued to listen, fascinated by every word he spoke.

"The most intense memories I have are the ones I've already told you about. When I was a little kid in that toy shop, I threw the biggest tantrum of my life. And then I blacked out. I had no idea at the time what was going on. But when I came to, the place was in darkness and all the lightbulbs were in bits on the floor."

He paused for a moment as he recalled the event.

"But that day when Ron was abusing my mom, and it was my birthday and he'd wrecked absolutely everything, I got so angry. I distinctly remember the heat in my head. That was all I was conscious of, an intense heat and this really strong need to hurt him somehow, to get revenge for all the trouble he'd caused. Next thing I knew, he was pinned against the wall and couldn't move."

"That was seriously scary!" he added before continuing. "It scared Ron enough to make him leave, but it scared me too. And my mom! That was when we both knew something was going on; that somehow I was causing these things to happen."

He took a deep breath and closed his eyes as he pictured the scene in his mind.

"From that moment on, Mom swore me to secrecy. She was petrified that if anyone found out, they'd take me away and she'd never see me again. People already thought we were weird, because of my mom being a psychic and all. But that was what she did for a living and if anyone found out about me, she thought they'd be too frightened to come near us. And we needed her income to survive."

"Is that why she freaked out when she saw us in the kitchen?" I asked quietly. I'd already known the answer to that question. It was obvious how she felt, but I wanted to hear the details from Sam.

"Yeah!" he admitted with a solemn nod. "It was supposed to stay our secret. Just between me and her. I've never told anyone else. That is…until you came along."

When he looked at me then, the shiver that ran down my spine was not an anxious one. It was not from fear or nerves or worry. But instead it came from a special place deep inside and somehow, I knew that Sam could feel it too. All I could do was smile back in return and promise to never, ever share his secret with anyone.

As I lay in bed, I pictured once more, the smile that had formed on his face at that moment; and I felt once again the flutter of butterflies in my stomach. It was a special, wonderful feeling that hours later, was still creating chills inside me.

Laying in my bed, the covers pulled up to my chin to ward off the cool breeze coming from the open window, I realized that I still had no idea how to move things with my mind. While I hoped to eventually learn the skill, I was no longer sure it was possible. But somehow, it didn't seem important anymore.

My last thought, before closing my eyes and drifting into a deep sleep, was that telekinesis was Sam's special skill and not something I needed to master. It was his power and his alone, and it was also a secret that I was determined would stay with me forever.

So different...

The next day was the day of our field trip to the science center and finally, before I left Sam's house the afternoon before, I'd managed to convince him to come along.

Apparently, though, it had taken some persuasion before his mom finally agreed to sign the permission note. She was angry over the kitchen incident and had threatened to ground him for a month. Apart from school itself, that included the field trip.

He said he'd argued that the science center visit was part of his schooling and because it was an educational trip she should let him go. I smiled to myself when he told me that. He'd previously had no interest in going at all and then all of a sudden, he was super keen. I knew I was responsible for changing his mind and thought that was pretty cool. But he also let me know his mom was scared I might tell people what I knew.

"I told her we had nothing to worry about," he explained. "And I told her that we could trust you."

Sam stared quietly towards me as he spoke those words. It was as though he was searching for final confirmation that I really would keep my promise.

Crossing my heart with an X, I stared back at him and shook my head. "I will never, ever tell a living soul."

"I know you won't," he replied solemnly as he sat back in his seat. "That's exactly what I told my mom."

Rather than convincing her himself though, according to Sam, it was his mother's own gut instinct that had persuaded her in the end. He said that she'd already formed her own opinion of me and that she was glad Sam and I had become friends.

"I'm glad too!" I grinned at him then, as I took in his words.

I was so relieved that his mom was ok with the two of us hanging out, especially now she was aware Sam had confided in me. I'd hate it if anything or anyone were to prevent us from spending time together.

As I settled back in my seat, I thought once more about how different Sam's mom was to my own. If only my mother was as accepting of other people as Mrs. Worthington was.

Instead of approving my new friendship with the boy who lived right next door, Mom was suspicious and she'd made that quite clear the afternoon before.

As soon as I returned from Sam's, I knew instantly she was not impressed. "So, what did you and Sam get up to all afternoon? She'd looked at me curiously, her eyebrows raised, waiting for my response. "You've certainly been gone long enough!"

Glancing sideways at her, I stood at the kitchen sink and began to peel potatoes in preparation for dinner. She was in a strange mood and I knew I had to be careful how I answered.

She'd always been very strict about who I hung out with. I guess that came with being an only child. I knew she was overprotective because she cared. But I wasn't a little kid anymore and surely by now, I could be allowed to make my own friend choices. And besides that, it wasn't as though I was hanging out at the mall doing things I shouldn't be. Her constant nagging about Sam was becoming annoying. I simply wanted her to like him and be happy there was someone right next door who I could spend time with.

I continued peeling as I spoke, keen to avoid eye contact. I certainly did not want her suspecting me of not telling the truth. But in this case, I had no choice.

"Not too much really. Sam's into computer games and we played some of those together. It was actually quite fun. He showed me a new one that I've never played before. I didn't even know it existed." I felt bad about lying to her. Luckily though, she believed every word.

"Well the last thing I want is for you to become hooked on computer games, Tess!" she frowned as she spoke. "I have friends who constantly complain about their kids being on the computer, playing one game or another. You have an important year ahead of you at school and you need to stay focused!"

"Don't worry, Mom," I sighed, discreetly rolling my eyes. "The games are fun but you don't have to worry about me becoming addicted. You know I've never been obsessed with that sort of thing."

"Well as long as that doesn't change," she added crossly as she passed me another potato.

"And I've been thinking…" she paused for a moment as if taking a moment to choose her words, "…if you're going to be spending so much time with that boy, we really should get to know his family. I think I'll invite them over for dinner on the weekend. I'll cook a roast chicken. Everyone loves my roast dinners."

"That sounds great, Mom," I replied, daring to look at her then, "except Sam's mom is a vegetarian. She doesn't eat chicken or any other meat!" I waited in anticipation for her reaction to that comment.

As expected, she let out an exasperated sigh. "Oh my goodness. Vegetarian! What on earth will I cook for them?"

"I don't know," I replied, trying to stifle a laugh. "I'm sure you'll come up with something. You might even discover some really nice meals that you've never tried before."

I did a silent cheer in my mind. The fact that Mom's master plan had been sabotaged, if only momentarily, was pretty funny and it took a concentrated effort not to laugh out loud. While I was sure she'd eventually choose one type of dish or another, in the meantime, Sam and his mom were off the hook.

As I continued peeling and chopping the variety of vegetables that were on the benchtop in front of me, I imagined all of us sitting around a dinner table together. My dad would probably be fine. Between my parents, he was the open-minded one and got along with pretty much everybody. But Mom was so conservative. She'd already commented on Mrs. Worthington's hippy style of clothing as well as the fact that she was a psychic. Mom found all of that quite strange. She was so different to our neighbor and I wondered what she'd find to talk about.

In contrast to my mother's opinion, I found Mrs. Worthington really interesting. I'd never met anyone like her before. And I actually looked forward to finding out more about her and what she did for a living. I would absolutely love to have her do a psychic reading for me. But then, when I thought about it some more, I realized perhaps that wasn't such a good idea. She'd probably pick up on my crush on Sam and who knows what else she'd find out. That'd be really weird and pretty embarrassing. I just hoped that she didn't know too much already!

Regardless of that, I considered the idea of moving next door to Sam and his mom the coolest thing that had ever happened to me. And that morning, as I sat on the bus with

Sam in the seat alongside me, I thought about how different my life had become.

Then, feeling a sudden urge to turn my head, I looked at Sam. And in true form, at the same moment, he turned to look at me as well. Aware of the quivering flutter in my stomach, the grin widened on my face, and at the sight of his own genuine heart-warming smile, my heartbeat quickened a little bit more.

The invite...

When we arrived at school, everyone was waiting in their
class groups ready to leave for the field trip. There was a
buzz of excitement about the day ahead and we could
hardly wait to get going.

Finally, our teachers marked the attendance roll, and we
were able to line up to board the bus. Lacey Jackson, one of
the girls in my group, had already asked Tahlia to sit with
her, so that left me free to sit alongside Sam. I ignored the
odd looks from my friends as they glanced at Sam alongside
me. I knew they were probably wondering why I was
hanging out with him, but I didn't care in the slightest. All I
could think about was the science center and how much fun
it was going to be.

However, I wasn't prepared for the roll to be called again as
we got on the bus. This meant we had to board in
alphabetical order. I realized instantly that because Sam's
name was at the end of the list, he'd be the last to get on.

"I'll save you a seat," I whispered to him when I heard my
name.

Because our class had lined up behind the other two classes,
by the time I made my way up the steps of the bus, I found
that most of the seats had already been claimed. I walked
down the aisle, searching for an available double seat but
soon found that only single seats remained.

Sighing in frustration, I decided to grab a place next to a girl
from another class who I didn't know. But just as I was

about to sit, a rather bossy girl named Gracie pushed me out of the way and quickly claimed the spot for herself. So I was forced to keep moving.

That was when I heard a familiar voice near the back, calling my name. "Here Tess. I saved a seat next to me."

When I looked to see who the voice was coming from, I spotted Jake Collins, a massive grin on his face as he patted the seat alongside him. He was definitely the last person I wanted to sit next to so I glanced desperately around in search of another spot. But everyone else seemed to be saving their spare seats for their own friends. I sat down with a sigh.

It was not a good start and when Sam got onto the bus and spotted me alongside Jake, his surprised expression made me feel worse.

Folding my arms, I looked everywhere but at Jake. At the same time, I could feel his eyes on mine. When the bus lurched forward and headed down the road, he was thrown abruptly sideways, falling against me. Cringing slightly, I moved my arm away from his, and laid it across my lap.

"So Tess, how have you been?" His question was harmless enough and when I saw his friendly grin, I could see he was simply trying to be nice.

"Pretty good," I replied with a nod of my head, and then looked in the other direction in an attempt to avoid further conversation.

I wasn't interested in chatting to Jake. I'd already decided the less I had to do with him, the better. But he obviously had a different plan in mind and had decided the bus trip was the perfect opportunity.

"So Tess," his expression became serious, and he stared directly at me as he spoke, obviously getting straight to the point. "Are you planning on going to the disco on Friday night?'

Instantly my stomach dropped in anticipation of what was coming next. I'd heard from my friends that he was intending to invite me and I knew exactly what was ahead, but being prepared wasn't helping me at all. And I wasn't sure how to respond.

I glanced uneasily towards him, trying to appear vague and disinterested, "Yeah, I was thinking about it," I replied, looking away once more.

"I heard you're not going with anyone?" he continued, not missing a beat.

"Nah," I said, this time firmly shaking my head. "I just prefer to go on my own."

"Oh, that's no fun!" he exclaimed with a grin. "How about you go with me?"

His words had tumbled out in a rush and by his confident manner, it was quite clear what word he was expecting in response.

But the only thing I seemed capable of doing was to shake my head once more. I wanted to tell him there was no way I'd go to the disco with him. I wanted to tell him that I thought he was a bully and I preferred to have nothing to do with him. But I was unable to say any of that. My usual outspoken manner deserted me. With him at my side, I felt intimidated and unsure. And so I stayed quiet, unwilling to say anything at all.

This did not have the effect I'd hoped. He completely misunderstood my meaning because he continued to grin as he waited confidently for me to answer.

Keen to get it over and done with, I took a deep breath and mumbled quickly. "No offense, but I just want to go on my own."

Feeling slightly bad, I watched his face drop.

The whole situation was extremely awkward and I just wished I could get off the bus and away from him. An uncomfortable silence followed and neither he nor I said another word.

I was glad that I'd got my message across but at the same time, I knew that he was not at all impressed. He was used to getting his own way, I was quite sure of that. At the same time though, I knew there'd be plenty of other girls who he could ask. I decided that if he really wanted someone to go with, it was his problem and he was just going to have to deal with it.

When the bus eventually pulled to a stop, I breathed a sigh of relief and stood up, joining the queue of kids in the aisle. Making eye contact with Sam, I gave him a small wave, which he acknowledged with a wave of his own. At the same time though, I could feel Jake's eyes boring into the back of my head as he stood impatiently behind me.

The Science Center

Once inside the Science Center, we were told that each class had to be organized into two smaller groups which would remain together for the entire day. This would allow us to easily view various exhibitions and take part in the many hands-on activities. When the groups were divided, I edged closer to Sam in an effort to make sure we ended up together.

To my relief, this was exactly what happened and as I'd hoped, Jake was shuffled into the other group. Thinking that everything was working out, after all, I followed the teacher's directions and headed with Sam and the other kids towards a nearby theater for a light energy presentation.

Just as I entered the room, I felt someone barge past me in a rush to claim one of the remaining seats. Looking up in surprise, I spotted Jake's familiar figure, his dark hair and orange T-shirt standing out in the crowd. Dismayed at the sight of him, I grabbed a seat in the middle alongside Sam who was already seated. At the same time, I wondered what Jake was doing there. I knew our teacher had placed him in the other group, and I had a sneaking suspicion he'd swapped groups without permission.

Putting him out of my mind, I sat back to enjoy the show. The main overhead lights had been switched off leaving the theater momentarily in darkness and then without warning, multi-colored fluorescent beams of laser light whipped across the room. They were coming from all directions and the effect was truly amazing. I sat in awe, watching as the lights constantly changed colors and effects. Then, with a dramatic and effective finish, it ended as quickly as it had begun.

The following presentation although not as spectacular, was still very interesting and I listened carefully as the presenter demonstrated a variety of light energy experiments. I was completely absorbed in what he was showing us when I noticed Sam fidgeting in his seat alongside me. He was rubbing his fingers through his hair and shaking his head as well as constantly turning around to look behind him.

"What's wrong?" I whispered quietly, as I glanced around, wondering what the problem was.

"Someone's throwing things at me!" he replied, the irritation clear in his voice. "But I'm not sure who's doing it."

Sighing with frustration, I took a good look around, knowing exactly who the culprit was. And sure enough, I spotted Jake sitting a couple of rows behind us. There was just enough light for me to make out the smirk on his face and although he was pretending to focus on the demonstration that was underway, I knew for sure it had to be him.

I glared at him for a moment but he refused to acknowledge me and his gaze remained on the stage. Right then there was nothing I could do except hope that he would stop. At that point, Sam seemed not to have noticed him, and I wanted to keep it that way. If he realized Jake was to blame, I had no idea how he might react.

Unfortunately though, I wasn't able to keep Jake's presence a secret for long. When the presenter asked for a volunteer to go down onto the stage, several hands in the audience shot up into the air. Various kids were chosen and one of them happened to be Jake.

Shaking my head with annoyance, I watched him make his way down the steps and onto the stage. Risking a quick glance at Sam, I saw his face light up with recognition. I also heard his loud sigh of frustration as he kept his eyes focused on Jake's every movement.

We watched as each volunteer took turns to assist with various experiments. When it was Jake's turn, his confident grin and cheeky manner instantly caused loud laughter from the audience. He was known for being the class clown and was obviously taking advantage of having everyone's attention. Clearly thriving on the response, he continued on with his silly manner until almost everyone seemed to be cracking up with laughter. Everyone except Sam and myself.

I no longer saw him as funny, although it seemed everyone else thought he was hilarious. He had this uncanny way of being a comedian without even trying, and I guessed that was what made him so popular. The more everyone laughed, the more he appeared to enjoy himself and the funnier he became. Even the presenter found Jake amusing and before he left the stage, he was congratulated for being such an entertaining volunteer.

Rolling my eyes skyward, I whispered quietly to Sam, "He makes me sick. I think I want to throw up!"

But Sam didn't reply. He just sat quietly and watched as Jake made his way back to his seat.

When the show was over, I waited for everyone else to file out, before standing myself. I wanted to put as much distance between Jake and the two of us as possible. That was when we both noticed handfuls of peanuts on the carpet around Sam's feet. At that stage, the theater was fully lit and we could see them scattered around the floor. They were obviously what Jake had been throwing, and clearly, he'd aimed well. Frowning at Sam, I stood quickly, not wanting him to dwell on the mess around him. Instead, I grabbed him by the arm and dragged him along behind me, chatting on about the laser light show in an effort to distract him.

By the time we reached the foyer area, it was a hive of activity and we had to search for the rest of our group. Spotting them heading towards an outdoor area, for a morning tea break, we had to run to catch up.

When we reached it, we noticed the sign that read, 'The Sundial Courtyard' and after quickly scanning the information, realized that it was a giant concrete steel and glass sundial that could be used to tell the time. Apparently, when the sun was shining, it was supposed to be quite accurate and when we checked, we found to our surprise that it actually was.

Spotting a couple of spare seats in a corner, I put my bag down and waited for Sam to join me. He was fascinated by the sundial's accuracy and was taking his time to check out the circular markings on the ground and the shadows that had been created.

Glancing around at the other kids, I spotted Jake on the other side sitting with a few of his friends. I guessed that was the reason he'd swapped groups and I could understand him preferring to spend the day with them. But when I caught him staring at Sam, I wasn't so sure if that was the real reason. After all, he had friends in the other group as well. I kept a discreet eye on him as he stared intently towards Sam, and it took a few moments before he realized I was watching. Then he looked abruptly away.

Deciding to ignore him, I called Sam over and offered him the container of chocolate chip cookies that I'd packed just for him. They were the ones that he'd tried before and I knew how much he liked them. Then to my surprise, he opened his lunch box and handed me a carefully wrapped slice of his mom's delicious carrot and walnut cake.

I was so thrilled that he'd thought to do that and beamed happily back at him. Not only did I love his mom's cake, it was the fact that he'd thought to bring me a slice that mattered the most. And as I scraped the creamy white icing off the wrapping paper with my finger, I happened to look across the sundial where Jake seemed to be watching our every move.

Aware of an uncomfortable premonition deep inside, I returned my focus to Sam and the delicious cake that I held in my hands. I was determined not to let Jake spoil our day. All we had to do was ignore him. If Sam could do it, then I was sure I could too.

At the same time, I had the distinct impression that I needed to stay alert just in case.

Highlights...

Our next stop was the Planetarium and the place that Sam and I were most looking forward to. We soon found that we were not disappointed. The best part was definitely the Cosmic Skydome where a realistic view of the galaxy had been created by a high-tech projector. We had so much fun trying to locate and name all the planets, stars, and constellations that were in view. It was incredible and so much better than anything I'd ever viewed through my telescope.

Unexpectedly, though, it was actually the next session that was the best part of the entire day. This was where we were able to explore all the really cool hands-on activities.

Our first activity was to trial throwing a baseball to test our speed and accuracy. My throw was pretty hopeless and we both laughed at my low score. We'd been watching the other kids and some of their throws were quite impressive. But when the captain of the school baseball team stepped onto the mat, it sparked an interest from everyone.

As he was also the team pitcher and renowned for how fast and hard he could throw a ball, we expected that his score would be way higher than anyone else's. Although he didn't beat the record which was recorded in lights on the board above the target, he still managed to easily outdo everyone else.

"I bet you could beat the record, Sam!" I grinned at him and nudged him with my elbow.

It was a half-hearted joke, but at the same time, I thought it really would be fun to test his skill and see how fast he could actually throw.

Raising my eyebrows, I gave him a nod of encouragement and continued. "Maybe you could try it just this once?"

Hesitating for a moment, Sam took a quick look around. When he realized that most of the other kids in our group had moved on and we pretty much had the area to ourselves, he made a split second decision. Picking up the ball, he stood at the start line, with the target lined up ahead of him. I watched, fascinated, as he threw the ball with all his strength. It flung rapidly into the air and made a bee-line for the target. But rather than falling short, it powered on and hit the target dead center with a pounding thump. The impact was so loud that several pairs of eyes turned our way.

Then we heard the loud reaction of a boy we didn't know as he raced over to check out the target. "Look at that huge dent!!!! You nearly destroyed it!"

From where I was standing, I could clearly see the indentation, and the ball that had dropped to the floor looked like it had actually burst open. I could not help my stunned expression as I stared at Sam. And then I noticed others looking at him in exactly the same manner. Grabbing him by the arm, I dragged him quickly into the next room, where we tried to hide amongst a crowd of kids engrossed in another activity.

"OMG! That was incredible!" The two of us cracked up laughing over what had just happened.

I knew it wasn't really a laughing matter, but neither of us could help it. Then when I noticed we were attracting attention once again, I tried to stifle my laughter.

"Sam! Did you see the dent in that target? That was crazy! You really should think about joining the baseball team, you know. They'd drool over someone as strong as you!"

"Ha Ha! Yeah, but nahhh! I'm not really into baseball," Sam laughed. "I've got to admit though, that was pretty fun!"

"Oh my gosh!" I exclaimed. "That was the best. Do you want to try it with something else?"

Now that we'd started, I had to see more. And with everyone around us so distracted, I thought that surely we could manage one more trial. Sam looked skeptically at me though, and I could see that he wasn't sure. But caught up in my excitement, he followed my lead.

"Maybe one more time wouldn't hurt," he grinned, looking around for something else to test his skill.

Then when his eyes fell on the steadiness tester, he nodded towards it. "That should be a pretty safe choice!"
The idea of this activity was to test how steady your hands were. To do so, you had to move a metal ring along a bar, without letting the two touch each other. We watched as a few kids had a turn. But no one was able to keep their hands steady enough for the ring to pass smoothly along without making contact with the bar.

When I had a go, I got the same result. I almost made it on the second attempt, but once again, the two metal objects touched…even though, I'd taken it as slowly as I could.

Then Sam stepped up, and within seconds the ring was at the other end. It looked to me as though he had barely touched the ring. In fact, he did it so fast, that he probably hadn't touched it at all, just made it look that way.

"That was too easy," he smiled, as we headed in a different direction, looking for something more interesting.

That was when we spotted Jake at the running track. This activity was called 'The Ten Meter Dash' and it timed your speed on the track. Once again, the record score was displayed in lights at the end of the track, next to the spot where the runner's speed was displayed.

Several kids were lined up to have a turn and standing amongst them was Jake. He was very fast, everyone knew that. He was the fastest on the football team and probably the fastest runner in the whole school. So we were all interested to see if he could beat the record.

Sam and I stood back to watch and when Jake stood at the start line, I caught him glancing towards us. With a smirk in our direction, he took off, running like lightning. While he didn't beat the record, his score was pretty high. He was in the top ten runners for the week and his time came in at number two.

"Second?" he queried in disbelief. "That can't be right. I want another go!"

He proceeded to push his way back to the top of the line. I could see the look of determination on his face as he ran. And it certainly paid off because this time his score moved to first place.

Everyone cheered when they saw the result, patting him on the back with admiration. For the second time that day, I rolled my eyes unimpressed. I wasn't unimpressed with his ability, but with his manner. He had such a big head and I was sick to death of the way he carried on.

When he caught us both watching him, he looked from Sam to me and then back to Sam again, deciding this was a perfect opportunity for some more humiliation. Somehow though, I think I was to blame for his sudden decision. Although, as usual, he chose Sam for his target.

"Hey Sam!" he called loudly. "Let's see how fast you can run!"

I turned towards Sam and saw that he'd turned a bright shade of red. It was the middle of the science center and just about every pair of eyes were upon him.

"Sam, just ignore him," I whispered, trying to tug him away. "Let's go somewhere else."

"There you go, getting girls to stick up for you! AGAIN!" he smirked, curling his lip in disgust. "She can probably run faster than you as well."

Laughing loudly now, he looked around, checking to see what response he was getting from everyone else. But they all stood still and stared. I felt Sam's movement. It was only slight, but I could sense that he was going to do something he shouldn't.

"Just let it go, Sam," I whispered, the anxiety in my stomach becoming worse by the second.

Rather than choosing to ignore Jake, Sam ignored me. "You're on!" he replied, staring at Jake. "And I bet I can beat your score!"

"Hahaha! That's hilarious!" Jake replied, clearly enjoying himself. "This I've gotta see!"

And without further hesitation, Sam stepped up to the mat, the kids who were already lined up there, happily made way for him. A competition was in place and everyone was interested in seeing the result.

At the sound of the bell Sam took off, and without even checking the timer, I could tell that he was fast. I'd had no idea that he could run, but then I wasn't sure if it was his telekinesis helping him or not. I knew he could move other objects around but did he also have the power to move his own body?

The thoughts swirled in my head as I watched the timer tick over. He reached the finish line in a flash and I saw immediately that he hadn't beat the record, but I wondered if he'd beat Jake. And staring in awe, I watched his score move up the board into first place.

The look of shock on Jake's face was the highlight of the day for me. I still don't know what enabled Sam to run so fast. Perhaps he is a true athlete with other skills hidden away that no one knows about. But if he wants to keep that fact secret, then that's his choice. Right then, I was content with witnessing Jake's humiliation.

And the smug grin that appeared on Sam's lips as he moved away was one he deserved. Hurrying after him, I felt my heart skip a beat. I was still learning about the boy who had become my friend. And as each day passed, I was growing to like him even more.

Plans...

Friday afternoon finally arrived. After the field trip, the main thing on everyone's mind was the disco that night. It was all we could think and talk about. However, Samantha and Tahlia could not believe I'd said no when Jake asked me to go with him.

"What?" Samantha had asked in surprise when she heard. "But why would you do that? Why would you say no?"

Before I had a chance to respond, Tahlia answered for me. "Because she likes Sam! She'd rather go with him. Isn't that right, Tess?"

Tahlia was grinning at me. I didn't think she meant any offense, she was just joking around. But even so, I felt a clenching sensation inside. Samantha was staring in disbelief as if she couldn't comprehend what she was hearing. And it seemed that Tahlia thought the idea of hanging out with Sam a big joke. I sighed in frustration and struggled to keep my opinions to myself.

But where Sam was concerned, I knew they'd never see my point of view. To them, he was weird and just not cool enough to be bothered with. If only they got to know him, just talked to him, they'd find that he wasn't weird at all. That would never happen though. They were only interested in being friends with the cool group, the popular kids of the grade.

As for Jake, apparently, he'd told everyone that he'd changed his mind and had decided to go to the disco on his own.

When Tahlia shared that piece of information, all I could do was roll my eyes.
"Whatever!" I'd whispered under my breath as I glanced towards him. He was sitting with a group of boys behind us and I could easily hear his loud voice above everyone else's.

We were all supposed to be working on a Geography project. Tahlia, Samantha, Lacey and I had been grouped together, but right then, we weren't getting too much work done. That day, we had a substitute teacher while Miss Browne attended a conference of some sort. The class was pretty noisy and when I glanced around, it seemed that most people were busy chatting…but not about the Geography project.

I caught Sam's eye from across the room. He'd ended up in a group with Jasmine and a couple of other nerdy kids. Miss Browne had previously arranged the groups, saying that she'd placed us in groups where she thought we'd work well. She was expecting us to complete most of the project that day, but from what I could see, there wouldn't be too many groups who would manage to do that.

Right then, our own group was focused on Lacey, who was describing the outfit she planned to wear that night.

I was listening half-heartedly, while still trying to decide what I was going to wear myself when I felt a thump on the back of my head.

"Ow!" I said, as I turned around crossly. "What was that?"

Jake, who was sitting right behind me gasped in surprise, "Oops! Sorry! That was an accident."

I frowned at him, unimpressed. I'd caught him tossing things my way in the past, and "accidentally" hitting me with them. It seemed that throwing things at people was a popular habit of his. This time though, it appeared his excuse was genuine because a boy called Tom, came over to retrieve an eraser that was lying on the floor beside me.

Obviously, Jake had been trying to pass it to him but had hit me in the head instead.

I ignored the two boys and returned my attention to Lacey, who was in the middle of describing the sequined jacket that she'd recently bought at the local shopping mall. It sounded really pretty and I was sure it would look great with the blue skinny jeans she was planning to wear that night. Out of the blue, Jake plopped down in a chair beside her and began listening in on the conversation. He grabbed a pen off my desk and tossed it around in the air.

"Jake, can I have my pen back please?" I held out my hand and waited for him to return it.

But rather than handing it straight back, he tossed it in the air a few more times and then put it on my desk before getting up and returning to his group. He was so annoying and ever since the field trip he'd become more annoying than ever.

"He's just trying to get your attention," Tahlia had told me more than once. "Seriously, you should just go out with him. You guys would be so cute together."

That thought just made me want to throw up. I couldn't understand why they liked him so much. All I wanted to do was avoid him.

Putting him out of my mind, I returned my attention to the girls and the conversation around me. I was caught up in their excitement and ever since Sam had agreed to go, I was looking forward to it even more.

Finally making a decision about what I would wear, I was impatient to go home and get ready. Taking a quick glance across the room, I caught Sam's eye and as usual, the wide smile that spread across his face caused familiar flutters in my stomach.

The disco...

It all started so well. Right from the moment I hopped off the bus and waved to Sam, telling him that I'd see him soon. I was filled with jittery excitement.

My outfit ended up being a perfect choice. And even though all the other girls were wearing new clothes, they admired my outfit more than anyone else's. Samantha and Lacey, in particular, continued to comment on how nice I looked and I was so glad I'd made the right choice after all.

The pale blue dress was one I'd bought the summer before and was still my favorite. It had a fitted band of elastic around the waist which was attached to a flared skirt below. And it matched perfectly with my little blue jacket. I loved the tabs that were held in place on the front of my jacket by small gold studs. Judging by the comments of the other girls, it was a great combination and I felt happier than ever.

The hall had been decorated with really pretty lights that flickered in the darkness. There was also a mirror ball hanging from the ceiling and a laser light set up in a corner of the stage. It flashed colored patterns that matched the various beats of the music. There was such a cool atmosphere and I loved the thrill of it all.

Although I was impatiently waiting for Sam to arrive, I stood amongst the others, all of us chatting excitedly as we watched everyone on the dance floor. Samantha, Tahlia, and a few other girls had their boyfriends sitting beside them. Even so, it made no difference to our group and I was grateful for that. I'd previously thought I'd be the only one not paired up but it hadn't worked out that way at all.

Later on, however, when the disco was over and I had a chance to think about what had happened, I wondered if the sequence of events could have taken a different path. If the night had gone according to plan then perhaps this may have been the case. But then, I guess I will never know. Because as fate would have it, things did not happen the way I expected them to.

Sam and I had originally planned to get a lift together. It was arranged for my mom to drop us off, but unfortunately, something came up and Sam called at the last minute to tell me he was running late and would see me there. He offered no explanation and I didn't ask. Although thinking back, that was the first in the chain of events. And of course, that led to the next circumstance, Sam's disappearance; another event that could easily have been prevented if only we had arrived together.

While waiting for Sam, I joined Tahlia a few times on the dance floor, although this was because she kept dragging me up to dance. But then if I hadn't been in that particular spot, I probably would not have noticed Sam's face at the door. Thrilled that he'd finally arrived, I continued dancing as I waited for him to make his way over. I was sure he'd spotted me but when I looked again, he had disappeared.

Thinking little of it, I kept dancing. It was a great song and Tahlia wouldn't let me leave the dance floor even if I wanted to. But when the song ended and still there was no sign of Sam, I decided to go looking for him.

When I realized he was nowhere to be seen I began to worry and went outside the hall in search of him. There were a few groups of kids standing around as well as some supervising parents making sure that everyone stayed in the vicinity of the hall. Deciding to check elsewhere, I turned to go back inside. And that was when I spotted Samantha and Lacey chatting with a couple of other kids outside the toilet block.

"Hey guys," I said, walking past them.

"If you're looking for Sam Worthington I saw him head around that way," Lacey called out to me, pointing towards the end of the building.

Frowning, I thanked her, but at the same time, thought it was an odd direction for Sam to go in, especially as it was in darkness and an out of bounds area. The only place that particular walkway led to, apart from the playground, was the senior sports shed. But then I figured that maybe a teacher had asked him to get some equipment for the DJ to use. He'd been organizing music games and at one stage, I'd heard him announce that a hula hoop dance competition would be starting soon.

Thinking that may be the explanation, I made a split second decision and decided to have a look. Aware that I didn't have permission to be heading that way, I glanced quickly back to ensure no teachers or parents were watching, and then raced in the direction that Lacey had indicated.

When I reached the sports shed, I found the door closed. So I grabbed hold of the handle and pulled. The area was very poorly lit and as the door wouldn't open, I assumed at first that it must be locked. Just as I was about to return to the hall, the blaring music stopped momentarily and all I could hear was the voice of the DJ announcing the next song. But that brief interruption in the music allowed me to hear the muffled voices coming from behind the door.

Certain that I recognized Sam's voice, I tried the handle once more. But it would not budge. Realizing that the door must be locked from the inside, a sinking feeling of dread began to fill my senses. But it wasn't until I heard the familiar sound of a second voice that the alarm bells rang in my head.

Banging loudly on the timber, I called Sam's name, "SAM! SAM! It's Tess, open up!"

When there was no response, I shoved on the door with my shoulder in an attempt to open it before calling once more, "SAM!! OPEN THE DOOR!!!!!"

Pressing my ear to the wooden surface, I tried to listen to the voices within. But the music had restarted and all I could hear was a muffled blur.

And then realization dawned. Just like a light bulb suddenly illuminating a darkened room, the hazy fog in my head cleared and I was able to see things as they truly were. Instantly aware, I felt my eyes open wide with recognition.

It was what happened next that now stays foremost in my mind.

Without warning, the door suddenly burst open and Sam stood staring at me. Behind him, I caught sight of Jake Collins, his face a mask of sheer terror.

***

Book 3

Mind Power

Tess...

What struck me more than the terrified look on Jake's face, was the calm manner in which Sam was standing there staring back at me. Rather than a mask of rage, which was what I would have expected to find, Sam's expression was quite the opposite.

It was as though he were in a trance of some sort, and he appeared to have no sense of what was going on around him. At the same time, Jake was cowering in a corner of the shed, not daring to move a muscle. Glancing upwards, I noticed a variety of tools and sports equipment hovering high in the air above Jake's head, and that was when I understood his fear.

Apart from the usual balls and hoops and other harmless items that are kept in a school sports shed, there were also other things floating there, equipment that was much more dangerous.

Without saying a word, Sam turned in Jake's direction, and as if responding to his silent commands, the equipment began to swoop and dive just missing Jake's head by mere inches.

I watched in horror as a javelin spear suddenly whipped into the air and flew at lightning speed towards him. Covering his face with his arms, he pushed himself further into the corner, desperately trying to avoid the weapon that was heading his way.
"SAM!!!!" I screamed loudly, "STOP!!!!"

Distracted by the sound of my voice, Sam's concentration faltered, and the javelin spear fell harmlessly onto the concrete floor at Jake's feet. All the other items dropped to the floor as well. And when I looked at Sam again, he appeared dazed and shaken.

I shook my head in dismay. "Sam, what are you doing? This is crazy!! You could have killed him!"

Taking advantage of the disruption, Jake jumped to his feet and rushed towards the door, managing to step past me rather than passing anywhere near Sam. I only caught a fleeting glance of the fear in his eyes as he raced outside. But I heard his threat, loud and clear.

It rang in the air and worried me more than anything else. "You're going to pay for this! You freak!!

And with that he disappeared into the darkness beyond, heading for safety amongst the crowd of kids who were still milling around the entrance to the hall a short distance away.

Quickly coming to my senses, I grabbed Sam by the arm and dragged him out the door, pushing it closed behind me. I had no idea why he and Jake were in the sports shed in the first place, but I didn't bother to ask. All I knew was that we needed to get away as quickly as possible. If Jake were to follow through with his threat, then both Sam and I would be in deep trouble.

To begin with, it was an out of bounds area and neither of us should have been anywhere nearby without permission. But if Jake told anyone what had happened, I dreaded to think of the consequences. The shed was in a shambles with balls, hoops, baseball bats, baseball gloves and a variety of other bits and pieces scattered everywhere. But I didn't dare risk taking the time to tidy the mess. We needed to get away from there quickly. Flicking off the light switch, I grabbed Sam by the arm, dragged him out the door and slammed it shut behind me.

Realistically, it was likely that no one would believe Jake's story, but so many kids had already labeled Sam weird and strange, they were probably capable of believing anything. Added to that, the shed looked like a tornado had whipped through it. And someone would have to be held responsible. When Mr. Dawson, the sports teacher, arrived on Monday and checked his precious shed, there would definitely be questions asked. He was renowned for being a neat freak and everything had its place on the shelves. Even if Sam and I tried to pack it all away, Mr. Dawson would be sure to notice if anything had been misplaced.

Glancing quickly around me, I led Sam in the opposite direction that Jake would have taken. I certainly didn't want to bump into him and I also didn't want anyone to see us suddenly appearing out of the darkness. Otherwise, when questions were asked on Monday, we'd be the prime suspects.

Sticking to the darkened path that led around the back of the hall, we finally reached a side door that led through to some bathrooms, a storeroom and a rear entrance to the building. The door was usually kept open through the day, and I just hoped that was still the case. But to my dismay, we found it firmly closed, and when I tried to turn the handle it wouldn't budge. Obviously, it had been locked to prevent kids from wandering out through that particular exit.

With a frustrated sigh, I turned to Sam, who was following along quietly behind me. "We're going to have to go around to the front. Let's just hope no one notices us."

Nodding his head silently, he did not say a word. I could tell he was just as overwhelmed by what had happened, as I was. I couldn't read his expression in the darkness, but I could see his eyes darting fearfully from side to side.

As we turned the corner of the building, we came face to face with a group of kids standing around laughing. Doing my best not make eye contact with anyone, I hurried past the group. At the sound of my name, however, I froze in my spot and was forced to turn towards the voice.

"Tess! Where have you been?" Tahlia smiled at me in surprise. "I've been looking for you everywhere!"

"Oh, um, it's really hot in the hall," I stammered. "I just needed to get some fresh air!"

Just as Tahlia opened her mouth to respond, Sam appeared alongside me and she raised her eyebrows curiously.

"Um, see you inside," I mumbled quickly, before she could ask any more questions.

Continuing to the entrance, I made my way into the noisy interior, with Sam following along close behind me.

Just when I thought we were safe, I suddenly felt a pair of hands grab my arm, and drag me into the middle of a conga line that was winding its way past us. Each kid had hold of the person in front of them by grasping onto their hips or the belt of their jeans, or just by clinging onto their shirt. And every person in the line seemed to be singing along to the words of the song blasting through the speakers.

"Come on, Tess, this is fun!" Lacey yelled in my ear, her eyes wide with excitement.

Shaking my head, I tried to break away but she would not release her grip. And so I was forced to continue on in the line of kids, dancing around the perimeter of the hall. By the time I returned to the spot where I'd left Sam behind, he was nowhere to be seen.

Finally escaping from Lacey and the others, I searched for Sam, scanning the mass of kids in front of me, the flashing lights shining on their faces and bodies as they danced and chatted. Everyone seemed to be having such a great time. It felt strange that I'd been a part of that group just a short while earlier. But that had all suddenly changed when I went in search of Sam.

With the scene I'd left behind in the sports shed still foremost in my mind, I thought about the possible consequences if I hadn't turned up when I did. It all seemed surreal, and I found it hard to believe that what I'd witnessed was not simply a dream of some sort.

At Lacey's insistence, I joined her, Tahlia and several others back on the dance floor. But I felt disconnected and struggled to enjoy the remainder of the night. Continually scanning the groups of kids around me, I hoped to spot Sam amongst them somewhere. But I found no trace and eventually gave up looking.

I also saw no trace of Jake, although for that I was grateful. I just hoped that Sam hadn't bumped into him. The thought of that scenario caused a cold tingle of fear to run down my spine.

It would surely have led to disaster.

Sam…

I couldn't stay at the disco any longer. As soon as Tess was dragged into that conga line with the other kids, dancing and winding their way around the hall, it was my chance to escape. I just wanted to get out of there.

I still thought Jake deserved everything I'd done to scare him. But it was no excuse for the way I acted. That was stupid and dangerous. And the expression on Tess's face when she yelled at me to stop, told me quite clearly how crazy she thought I was.

As I waited impatiently on the curb with the loud music from the hall spilling out onto the street, I felt like such a loser. Although I should've been used to feeling that way, it didn't help make the situation any better.

When our familiar red sedan pulled up in front of me, all I wanted was to get home to the sanctuary of my bedroom so I could hide away in private where I belonged.

But first I had to deal with my mom's interrogation. And she quizzed me all the way home.

"How was it tonight?"
"Did you have fun?"
"Did you meet up with Tess?"
"It's pretty early to be going home. I would have thought you'd stay until the end?"
"Is there something wrong, Sam?"
"Didn't you have a good time?"
"Mom!" I exploded, "Stop with all the questions!"

When I caught the surprised expression on her face, it only added to my distressed state. Already overwhelmed with guilt, I stared towards her.

"I'm sorry," I sighed, "Yeah it was good. I'm just tired, that's all. I wanna get home to bed."

She glanced at me then, that knowing look on her face. And I shook my head at her in frustration. The worst part about having a psychic for a mom was the fact that she often knew what I was thinking. Sure, she asked a lot of questions. But she already knew the answers. Most of them anyway. I just hoped she didn't pick up on what had happened with Jake. If she knew all those details, I'd never hear the end of it.

I'd made endless promises that I wouldn't use my powers outside the house. She knew how strong they were becoming, and that was what worried her. But it worried me too. The problem was though, I had no idea how to deal with it.

When I finally reached my room, I sat on my bed and stared out the window into the darkness beyond. Filled with more frustration than ever, I shook my head in despair.

"I can't believe I was so stupid!" I muttered the words angrily, then picked up a school textbook that was laying on top of my desk, and hurled it forcefully at the wall.

The book hit the solid surface with a loud thud before falling to the floor. Of course, I hadn't picked it up with my hand and thrown it. That was what any normal kid would do. But I wasn't normal. And that was the cause of my problems.

All I had to do was become the slightest bit angry, annoyed, or frustrated, and then my invisible mind power did the rest.

For small objects, I didn't even need strong emotions to make them move. A glance in the object's direction was all that was necessary. Once the thought was in my mind that was all it took. As if by magic, the object transferred to wherever I wanted it to go. It was as simple as that. And it seemed that as I grew older, my skills became more and more powerful.

Sighing heavily once more, I stared at the book laying on the floor in front of me. That was what had caused all the trouble earlier. My telekinetic powers. The powers handed down to me by a freak of nature. Some may consider it a gift, and although it was definitely cool to be able to move things around with mind power alone, it also caused many problems.

Hours after the incident with Jake, I could still feel the intense heat that had appeared in my head.

I despised Jake more than anyone I had ever known; even more than my mom's old boyfriend, Ron. To me, Jake was the meanest, cruelest kid in the entire school, and the thought of the constant smirk on his face made my skin crawl.

I knew that he deserved what had happened earlier. And I had a feeling that Tess knew it too. But the look of shock on her face still made my stomach churn with worry. The last thing I ever wanted was for her to become scared of me. And tonight she was scared. I saw it in her eyes. That was what made me stop. If she hadn't been there, I have no idea what would have happened.

The thoughts raced around and around in my head, as I sat stock still on my bed, staring towards the window and the blackness outside.

Tess...

When my mom arrived to pick me up, I hopped into the car alone. It had been the plan for both Sam and me to catch a ride home together, but he had disappeared long before. I only hoped that he'd called his mom and made it home safely.

As the car turned into our driveway, I glanced through the bushes that separated Sam's property from ours and saw glimpses of light shining through the darkness. When I climbed the stairs to my room and looked out my bedroom window, the denseness of the trees prevented a clear view. But I knew that the streaks of light shining through the bush came from Sam's room.

Before drawing the curtains closed, I stared through the glass and wondered what he was doing right then. Had he made it home without encountering Jake? Was he bothered by what had happened? And was he worried at all about trying to control his powers and everything he was capable of?

These were questions I wanted answers to. I just hoped that I'd get the chance to ask them. He had left so suddenly and without a word. I felt disappointed that he hadn't even said goodbye. All the magic and excitement that I'd felt when I first arrived at the disco had disappeared along with him. I'd lost all interest and just wanted to go home as well.

With a deep sigh, I pulled my curtains closed and turned towards my bed. Then on a sudden impulse, I sat down at my computer desk and turned on my computer. While I waited for it to start, I thought some more about the scene

I'd witnessed earlier.

Jake's fear had been real. Of that, I had no doubt. And I wondered if perhaps that would finally put a stop to his endless bullying. No one had ever stood up to him before. His friends thought he was cool and followed along, while everyone else tried to stay out of his way so they wouldn't become his next target.

Although I did speak up once, I felt that I could have tried harder. Teachers continually reminded us that watching bullies in action and allowing the behavior to continue, was as bad as the bullying itself. And I tended to agree. But in reality, I felt that no one had the courage to do that, especially where Jake was concerned.

Although a few teachers had spoken to him at one time or another, it had barely made an impact. Jake was too smart and simply made sure that no teachers were around to see him in action. I knew that Sam's behavior was dangerous but I could hardly blame him. He had put up with too much for too long and Jake's constant taunting had to be stopped somehow.

When my computer screen lit up in front of me, I moved my finger over the mouse pad and did a Google search for the game that Sam had told me about. Clicking the link inviting new users to join, I filled in my details and set up an account. I wasn't sure if I'd be able to message Sam or not but decided to give it a try. Some of the girls at school played those games and had told me about the cool messenger function which they used all the time.

Sam didn't own a cell phone and I knew he didn't have any social media accounts. So I figured this might be a way to get a message through to him to make sure he was okay.

I had already turned my bedroom light off, so my parents thought I'd gone to bed, and I sat in the glow of the light from the computer screen. If my mom found me on the computer at that time of night she'd be really angry. I'd probably be banned from the computer for a week.

Deciding that my bed would be a safer place, I picked up my laptop and hopped under the covers, ready to instantly close the lid and pretend I was asleep if I heard my bedroom door suddenly open.
It was my mom's habit to check on me last thing at night, but as she had been heading to bed herself as soon as we got home, I was hoping she was already asleep. Knowing my mother so well though, I had to be careful.

After typing in Sam's username, I hit the search key. There was only one user with the name MindFreak, which was the name I remembered him telling me about. I also recalled thinking that it was an appropriate name for him to use. Although I didn't think of him as a freak in any way, it was still a cool sounding name, and his mind powers were definitely freaky.

At the time, he'd tried to convince me to join the site so we could compete against each other in his favorite game. I'd laughed and said that computer games like the ones he played weren't something I'd never tried before. And he smiled as he tried to persuade me. "But this game is so much fun, Tess. You should try it sometime!"

I said that I would, but ended up forgetting about it. I'd thought no more about it until that night. And right then, it seemed the perfect way to try to contact him. Clicking on the messenger link, I began to type my message....

Hey! This is Tess. Are you ok?

Leaning back on the pillows that were propped up behind me, I waited hopefully for a response.

Sam...

It was all Jake's fault. If he hadn't lured me down that path, it would never have happened.

I pictured the scene as it had unfolded after my arrival at the hall. The events played on fast forward in my mind, minute by minute just like the scenes of a movie. And as though I had stepped back in time, I relived it all over again.

"Hey, Sam," Jake said quite innocently as I walked past. "Are you looking for Tess?"

I turned towards him in surprise.

The fact that he was even speaking to me in such a civil tone, should have made me instantly suspicious. But I was so keen to find Tess that it hadn't registered in my brain at all

"I saw her go down that way," he said in a serious tone.

There hadn't been a hint of his usual smirk or arrogant manner. And so I believed him. And I headed ignorantly in the direction he'd indicated.

It was probably only a few seconds later that I heard footsteps. And I knew instinctively that he was right behind me. For some reason, I could sense it. Turning back to check had been my mistake. Although I knew that something was not quite right, he still managed to catch me off guard. And his almighty shove sent me falling heavily back onto the concrete path. Hours later, I could still feel the lump on the back of my head.

That was when my anger began to surface. I was at the disco to hang out with Tess and have some fun. And he was getting in my way. Tess and I were supposed to get a ride there together, but my mom made me wait until dinner was cooked, and that had taken forever. I didn't want to hold Tess up, so I told her I'd meet her there. That had been the plan.

And then Jake had to go and ruin it.

When I got to my feet and he shoved me backward, causing me to fall on my butt once more, I lost all control. The sports shed was right beside us, and with very little effort on my part, the door suddenly flung open with a loud bang. Luckily the loud music from the disco camouflaged the noise and no one heard a thing. But when I looked inside and saw the dark space, I knew it was my chance.

I'm still not sure how I managed to get him through the doorway. That part remains a mystery. All I remember was the two of us, suddenly inside the shed and the door slamming shut behind me.

Turning towards the door, I stared at the light switch and watched it flicker on. Then I looked back at Jake, who was frozen to the spot, his mouth gaping wide in shock.

I recalled the smug grin on my own face right then. For a change, it was me who was in control. The sight of him freaking out was the best thing I'd ever seen. Without all his gang around to boost him on, he was putty in my hands. An utter coward who couldn't even stand up for himself. Seeing him so helpless gave me more power than ever.

That's pretty much all I remembered though until Tess suddenly appeared at my side. It was so strange to see her there. She was like a vision at first, an image I'd conjured up out of nowhere. But then I saw the fear in her eyes, and I knew instantly that she was as real as her fear.

And when her piercing scream cut through the thick fog in my head, I finally came to my senses.

Will she ever speak to me again? Have I wrecked my chances and ruined our friendship forever? Am I the biggest loser in the universe for destroying the first special friendship I've ever had?

Shaking my head in despair, I got to my feet and picked up the book that still lay on the floor by my bedroom wall, and returned it to its spot on my desk. Then I moved to the window and stared out into my lonely, lonely world.

Tess, the first real friend I'd ever really had…what will happen to our friendship now?

Wallowing on my bed in a pool of misery, I was suddenly distracted by the beeping sound of a message on my computer.

With a deep and uninterested sigh, I got to my feet to find out who it was from.

Tess...

I felt a flutter of excitement at the unique sounding tone on my computer. And when I saw Sam's response pop up on the screen in front of me, I smiled happily.

MindFreak > *hey!*

I waited and watched as he continued to type until finally the rest of his message was in view.

MindFreak > *I'm fine. How r u?*

Breathing a sigh of relief, I typed my reply.

Tess > *I'm good*

MindFreak > *sorry about tonight*

I looked at the words on the screen and my heart melted. I completely understood why he'd acted the way he had. Jake deserved every bit of what had happened. And although he could have been badly hurt or even worse, I just hoped that it would put an end to his bullying and we could all move on. It didn't need to ever happen again.

Tess > *it's ok. I understand*

I had to wait a moment for his response to that. And after a minute or so with no reply, I wondered if he was going to respond at all.

Tess > *r u still there?*

MindFreak > *yeah*

Tess > *r u and ur mom still coming for dinner tmw nite?*

MindFreak > *if we're still invited?*
I grinned at that comment.

Tess > *of course ur still invited!*

MindFreak > *cya tmw nite then* ☺

Tess > cya tmw nite then ☺ ☺

And with a contented grin spreading across the width of my face, I clicked the sign-off link and shut down my computer.

Closing the lid, I picked up my laptop and placed it on top of the chest of drawers that sat beside my bed. Then I laid down and pulled the covers up to my chin. When I glanced towards my window, I could see the bright glow of the moon shining through the curtains. And beyond the trees, I was sure Sam still remained in front of his computer, probably playing his silly game.

With the wide grin still attached to my face, I closed my eyes and rolled onto my side. Seconds later, I had fallen into a deep sleep.

Sam...

At first, I was confused when I heard the message alert on my computer and saw the unfamiliar username. I'd never seen that username before although new names popped up all the time, they were never people's real names.

It took a moment for the thought to register, but when I realized who the message was from, I felt a crazy butterfly type sensation in the pit of my stomach.

It was so unexpected that I was struggling to believe it was real. For a moment I wondered if someone was playing a trick, but somehow I knew that wasn't the case.

So I clicked on the message icon. And as soon as I saw the words...*'Hey! This is Tess. Are u ok?'* my stomach seemed to flip out inside me. Like a crazy ride at an amusement park, it was doing cartwheels at the realization that my neighbor, the girl who I couldn't stop thinking about, had actually messaged me via my favorite gaming website.

I held my breath as I typed my reply, and felt so nervous that it took forever for the words to appear properly on the screen. I kept making mistakes and had to delete what I'd written and start all over again.

And then the messages had appeared, one after the other. It was like a magical dream...but instead of a dream, I really was chatting online with the girl who I had a serious crush on.

The message from her that stood out the most was...*It's ok. I understand*

When I read those words, I was flooded with relief, and the relief was so strong that I felt like whooping for joy.

I hadn't wrecked our friendship. She didn't think I was a loser. And she still wanted us to go to her house for dinner the following night. When I climbed into bed a little later, I still could not believe my luck.

Tess was the coolest, most genuine person I'd ever met. And I vowed never again to scare her the way I had earlier. To jeopardize our friendship, was just plain dumb. No one was worth risking that. And especially not a bully like Jake Collins.

Finally, the sickening nausea that had overwhelmed me earlier had disappeared, and in its place was a happy, contented feeling that everything was going to be okay.

But perhaps I shouldn't have been so sure. Before my online chat with Tess, I'd always been on edge, aware of what and who was around me. It was a kind of self-preservation that I'd developed over the years; my only way of coping with my everyday existence.

If I hadn't let my guard down, I would have been better prepared for what lay ahead. And I soon found out, that would be my downfall.

Tess...

From the moment I woke, I was worried about our planned dinner with Sam and his Mom. Although I was happy they were coming over, I kind of wished that they weren't.

Amongst other things, my mother was in a panic over what to cook. She really didn't need to make such a big deal of it all, but the idea of a vegetarian menu was making her more and more and stressed. It was as though she felt she had something to prove, and I couldn't understand why she was in such a state. I tried to help out with suggestions but it seemed that none of them were good enough.

"That sounds disgusting!" was her comment about one particular recipe that included red kidney beans. "I wouldn't even know where to buy those, and besides, your father would never eat that!"

"How about a vegetable curry?" This was my second suggestion and what I thought was quite a good one.

"Spicy food will not agree with my sensitive stomach, Tess. You know the doctor said I should avoid spicy foods!"

After several more ideas, she was still dissatisfied and almost ready to call the whole thing off. In frustration, she pulled out an old recipe book that had a small vegetarian section, and then finally decided on vegetarian lasagna.

I rolled my eyes when she told me that. "Mom, vegetarian lasagna was one of the first meals I suggested. But you said it was too difficult."

"Oh I don't remember saying that," she replied with a frown. "It's fiddly to make but I didn't realize you could make it without meat! Vegetarian lasagna is a great idea!"

Clearly pleased with herself for finding the perfect choice, she returned to the kitchen to make a list of all the necessary ingredients.

I shook my head at her and sighed, but at least she'd finally settled on something she was happy with. I just hoped that her vegetarian version tasted okay. She was definitely not a master chef, and the idea of my mom putting something together that she'd never baked before was a concern.

For dessert, I was planning to bake brownies. My brownies were a favorite in our household and seemed the perfect choice. I wasn't sure how'd they compare to ones that Mrs. Worthington might make, as her baking was the best, but I hoped that both Sam and his mom would be impressed.

I really wanted the night to be a success but the food we served for dinner was only a part of what worried me.

My main worry was my mother's attitude towards 'hippies' and alternative types of people, and Mrs. Worthington certainly fitted into that category. I knew my dad would be no problem, but my mother was so conservative and opinionated. I just hoped she wouldn't be too embarrassing.

As the day passed by, I became more and more nervous. It had begun when I jumped out of bed that morning and remembered what was ahead. Although I couldn't wait to see Sam again, I just hoped that everything went smoothly. But instead of focusing on what could go wrong, I eventually decided to change my attitude and focus on positive thoughts instead.

To begin with, I was relieved that Sam and I were still on good terms. When he left the disco without a trace, I wasn't sure if he'd ever want to face me again. It was hard to know how his mind really worked, but I suspected he'd be embarrassed about what had happened and not sure how I would react.

Apart from being dangerous, his behavior was not what anyone would call normal. And I knew that was what he feared the most. As cool as his powers were, I was convinced that he wanted to fit in. Although he didn't admit it, I was sure that his must be a lonely existence

I thought about the comments I'd heard from Jake and his friends and knew how hard it must be for Sam to face that every day.

"He's such a freak!"
"OMG…he's seriously weird!"
"That kid creeps me out!"

Admittedly, most of those comments came from Jake, but I heard other kids whispering similar things to each other. It wasn't fair. Sam had done nothing to deserve that.

To me, he was not at all weird or strange or spooky. Instead, I thought he was the coolest person I'd ever met. And rather than being scared of his powers, I wanted to learn more about them. I was also curious to know what else he was capable of. And I was not going to let the other kids' opinions change mine.

My mom had always said that I had a mind of my own. "Ever since you were little, you were so strong-willed and independent!"

She often made that statement, usually when we were in the midst of an argument and I refused to see things her way. She also complained about my determined personality and how difficult she found it to deal with. But as far as I was concerned, she just needed to open her mind to possibilities and accept people for what they were.

I thought about her recent outburst after another of our many arguments. "I hope you're not going to become one of those rebellious teenagers. Because there is no room for that sort of behavior in this house!"

My dad simply raised his eyebrows at that comment, and then returned his attention to the newspaper in front of him. He knew better than to argue with Mom. But at least I knew he was on my side. We just seemed to click, my dad and I. And I was so glad to have him around.

I was also grateful to have his support for the night ahead, and I made a point to speak to him about trying to keep Mom's prying questions in check.

However, I should have known that would be a difficult task. Because my mother was also very strong-willed, and never afraid to speak her mind or say what she thought about any given topic. And try as I might to remain positive, my mother's outspoken opinions were what worried me the most.

Sam...

As soon as I woke up, I thought of her. And the first place I looked when I opened my eyes was towards the open window near my bed. The curtain fluttered in the morning breeze and I could hear the noisy squawk of birds as they swooped and darted in search of a tasty breakfast.

Even though I usually went to bed late, I always woke early. I guessed that was partly from habit and partly from the morning sunlight that streamed through the window. The sheer fabric of the curtain did little to prevent the morning light from pouring into my room. But I didn't mind. I enjoyed the brightness and warmth of the sun. It was the one cheery thing that I woke up to on cloudless mornings.

That was until I'd met Tess.

She was the one who now featured in my mind. And the fact that she accepted me for who I was, meant more to me than anything. Finally, I had a friend I could trust and share my innermost, darkest secrets with. Even though I was not part of the cool crowd at school and my mom and I were not what anyone would call normal, she didn't seem to care. And most importantly, I hadn't scared her away.

The scene from the sports shed filtered through my thoughts, and for about the hundredth time since it happened, I grinned at the satisfying sight of Jake Collins, finally being put in his place. The vision of him trying to hide in a corner like some type of threatened animal, and escape the power of the person in front of him gave me the biggest thrill of all.

No longer did I feel like the victim, the kid who was alienated from everyone else, because Jake had zoned in on me as his target.

As I sat up in bed, I felt a strength that I'd never known before. I guessed it was a sense of power. Not the physical power that guys like Jake had due to their sheer size and weight. It was more of a mental power, one that I was sure could dominate any physical strength, even Jake's.

I'd finally come to realize how amazing my secret was. And it wasn't just the fact that I could move things with my mind. It was the inner confidence it had given me that made the difference.

Having Tess to hang out with definitely helped, but added to that, my power over Jake made me feel less of a loser. Previously, I dreaded being anywhere near him. Whenever that happened, he'd jump at the chance to humiliate me. Anything for attention from his mass of followers and fans; those stupid kids who called themselves his friends and who had nothing better to do than follow him around.

But in the blink of an eye, I'd changed all that. I was pretty sure that he'd think twice before bugging me again. At least I hoped that was the case.

However, I hadn't counted on Jake's huge ego and what he was actually capable of. That was something I was yet to encounter, and unfortunately, I soon found out that it was something I was not prepared for.

But right then, I didn't even consider that issue. Instead, I focused on the special night ahead. I could barely wait for the day to pass so I could see Tess again. Glancing quickly at the clock by my bed, I did a mental calculation…twelve hours and forty-two minutes to be exact, and I would be at her door.

That moment could not come quickly enough.

Tess...

When Sam and his mom arrived, I opened the door to greet them. My stomach was a bundle of nerves as I invited them in. Sam grinned at me shyly, but his mom's friendly manner quickly put us both at ease.

Mrs. Worthington was carrying a beautiful looking cake that she had baked especially, and she handed it to me with a smile.

"Oh my gosh, thank you so much!" I smiled in return. "This looks delicious! I made brownies as well, so we'll definitely have plenty for dessert!"

"Thank you for the invitation, Tess. We've been looking forward to this all week, haven't we Sam?" She turned towards her son, whose face immediately began to flush a bright shade of red.

Pretending not to notice, I led them down the hallway to the living room where my mom and dad were waiting. I saw my mother discreetly take in the sight of Mrs. Worthington, who was dressed in a gorgeous flowing dress in the most beautiful shade of lavender. It complemented her skin tones beautifully. And I couldn't help but notice the row of pretty feathery bracelets that decorated her arms. They also matched the ones that were tied delicately around her ankle. It was such a cool look and I wondered for a moment if she had made the jewelry herself.

The difference between the two women was immediately obvious and I took in the boring pearl necklace that hung around my mother's neck, as well as the plain blue dress that she'd chosen to wear. Their styles were so opposite. However, Mrs. Worthington didn't seem to notice. Or if she did, she didn't let it show.

I silently willed my mother to be polite. Gulping nervously, I tried to think of something to say, "I hope you guys like vegetarian lasagna. Mom has been busy in the kitchen all day. I'm sure it'll be delicious."

"That sounds wonderful," Mrs. Worthington beamed. "Lasagna is Sam's favorite, but I rarely make it because it's such a fiddly dish. Thank you for going to so much trouble, Janice."

Breathing a sigh of relief, I saw my mom's face and shoulders relax. The compliment from Sam's mom had put a pleased smile on her face.

"Well, I hope you enjoy it. I've never tried a vegetarian variety before, so let's hope it is okay. Please come in and sit down." She indicated the couches that lined the wall of the living room.

"Tess, would you and Sam like to get some drinks for everyone," Mom continued. "The fruit punch should be chilled by now. Would you like a glass, Fiona? Or would you prefer a glass of wine?" She indicated the glass in her hand, which I noticed was almost empty and which she would probably soon refill.

Wine was something she seemed to have taken a huge liking to lately, and I had a sense of impending doom at the thought of her drinking too much.

"Fruit punch sounds delicious!" Mrs. Worthington smiled.

Glad for a chance to escape, I grabbed Sam by the arm and pulled him into the kitchen. "Oh my gosh, my mother is so awkward!"

Sam laughed, "Mothers can be really embarrassing!"

"Your mom is great!" I replied, and then with a shake of my head, I added, "It's my mother who's the problem!"

I chatted a little with Sam while he watched me pour drinks for each of us. I avoided mentioning the disco, however, and decided we could talk about that later. There were a few things Sam needed to know before we went back to school on Monday. And I just wanted to make sure he was prepared.

With the glasses of fruit punch on a large tray, Sam carried them into the living room where our parents were deep in conversation. Surprisingly enough, they all seemed to be getting along quite well.

When I glanced at my dad, he gave me a small wink and I grinned back. I'd pleaded with him earlier to try and keep Mom's comments under control, and not let her say anything too embarrassing. So far, it appeared to be working.

It wasn't until later that my mother's true personality began to show. And the more wine she drank, the more outspoken she became. I should have realized that she wouldn't be able to control herself and that it would only be a matter of time.

Tess...

The lasagna turned out to be a huge success. Everyone enjoyed it, including Sam and his mom. And although my mother kept commenting on how difficult life must be as a vegetarian, she appeared to enjoy the meal as well.

It wasn't until dessert time when my brownies and Mrs. Worthington's cake were served, that Mom began to speak her mind.

"Hmmm, carrot cake? How unusual! I would never have thought of adding carrots to a cake!"
I jumped in quickly at her ignorant comment. "Mom, carrot cake is delicious. And Mrs. Worthington makes the best cakes. I'm sure you'll love it!"

She frowned at me in response to that and I realized abruptly that I'd said the wrong thing. Throughout the meal, I'd been raving about how creative Mrs. Worthington was and I wondered if my mom was feeling a little put-out.

I guess it was obvious how highly I thought of Sam's mother. As well as that, she and I had been chatting easily throughout the meal, while everyone else had tended to sit back and listen. I found her very easy to talk to. I just loved her easy-going manner and felt very relaxed around her. Whereas my mother was always so formal and particular, and I had to watch everything I said.

Sometimes I wondered how Mom and I could even be related. We were so different to each other, and lately, we seemed to be drifting further and further apart.

When she began asking the dreaded questions that I knew she'd be sure to bring up at some stage, my stomach clenched anxiously.

"So, Fiona, tell us about this psychic ability of yours? Apparently, you can tell people their future!" She looked directly at Mrs. Worthington who raised her eyebrows in surprise at Mom's tone.
Mom chuckled loudly at her own remark and it was obvious to everyone that she thought the whole idea was quite

ridiculous.

"Ah, Janice, I'm sure Fiona is very good at what she does," Dad interrupted, glancing at Mom with a frown. "I'd love to have a reading done some day Fiona. It's something I've always found fascinating."

Mrs. Worthington smiled at Dad gratefully, but her reply was quickly interrupted by my mother's next comment.

"Do you use a crystal ball? Like the type they have in the old movies? Is that how you tell people what's ahead for them?" She was laughing even more, clearly finding herself amusing.

Taking a deep breath, I glanced across the table at Sam, who was looking uncomfortably down at his plate. Everyone had a half-eaten dessert in front of them, but had abruptly stopped eating. My own appetite had drained away and was replaced with a nauseous sensation, the thought of more food making me feel ill.

"Ah, no," Mrs. Worthington replied politely. "That's not quite how it's done."

"She uses tarot cards!" Sam spoke up defiantly. He'd been fairly quiet until that point but had suddenly jumped in to defend his mother. "You should try it some time. You might be surprised about what she can tell you."
"Tarot cards did you say? What on earth are they?" Mom laughed once more and picked up her wine glass to take another sip.

As if that wasn't bad enough, her next comment was worse than ever. "Do people actually believe what you tell them, Fiona? Seriously, it's all a bit far-fetched, don't you think? A bit of a joke really."

I looked at Mom, horrified. I didn't think I would ever forgive her for humiliating me the way she was doing right then. I just wanted her to stop talking. Looking towards my dad for help, I caught his dismayed expression as he opened his mouth to speak.

But he was abruptly cut off by a sudden loud shriek that burst from my mother.

All eyes turned in her direction, where she sat open mouthed and in shock. Staring at the pool of wine that had spilled from her overturned glass, she watched helplessly as the pool of liquid dripped from the tablecloth and into her lap.

"Oh my," she gasped, a confused look on her face. "How did I do that?"

Rolling my eyes in disgust, I passed her a napkin, all the while shaking my head at her. She was so embarrassing!

Right then, however, an idea occurred to me. It came out of nowhere but I could not resist the urge to look at

Sam, who was sitting quietly staring at my mom while she tried to mop up the mess. His expression was filled with smug satisfaction and I knew instinctively what must have happened.

I stared at him in surprise, finding it hard to believe that he had just caused her wine to spill. Then, trying my hardest to suppress a laugh, I covered my mouth with my hand and suggested that Mom go and change.

Like an obedient child, she stood up from her seat and made her way to the stairs leading up to her bedroom. And with her gone from the table, the tension in the room disappeared. That was when I caught the hint of amusement in Mrs. Worthington's eyes, and I wondered if she was also aware that Sam had caused the glass to fall over.

As if in answer to my question, she turned towards me and winked. Right then, I thought that she was the coolest mother ever!

Dad managed to change the subject and get everyone chatting again by mentioning my telescope and the mutual interest that Sam and I shared.
"When we finish this delicious dessert, you'll have to try it out," he suggested to Mrs. Worthington. "That telescope is so high-powered, it's amazing what you can see on a clear

night. And when I looked outside earlier there wasn't a cloud in the sky."

Mrs. Worthington eagerly agreed, and as soon as everyone finished eating, we took her upstairs so she could see what we'd been talking about. True to Dad's word, we found the night sky clearer than it had been in a long time and Mrs. Worthington was in complete awe at what she could see. When they eventually decided to head home, I breathed a sigh of relief that the night hadn't ended in complete disaster.

But, I hadn't had any opportunities to chat alone with Sam, and I had so much to talk about. Racing quickly up to my room, I turned on my computer.

Sam...

My mom wasn't exaggerating when she told Tess we'd been looking forward to dinner with her family. Invitations to other people's houses didn't come along very often, so it was kind of a big deal for us to be invited. Apart from that though, I was just keen for an excuse to hang out with Tess.

But even so, I hadn't expected Mom to announce the fact that I couldn't wait to go there. That was really embarrassing.

Being embarrassed was something I was used to though. Before that night, I considered my mom the most embarrassing person in the world. Having a mother who wore strange hippy style clothing and worked as a psychic for a living was definitely not the norm, and most people found it really weird.

But I'd just discovered that in the scheme of things, my mother's embarrassing features rated fairly low. Especially when compared to Tess's mother. I didn't think that anyone could compete with how bad she was. And I soon found that Tess felt exactly the same way.

The moment I walked into my room and rebooted my computer, I spotted a message alert flashing on the screen. When I logged onto my account, and searched my messages, Tess's name popped up straight away.

Tess > *OMG! I can't believe you did that!*

MindFreak > *did what?*

Tess > *u know!*
MindFreak > ☺

Tess > *she deserved it…she was so rude. I'm really sorry!*

MindFreak > *I'm sorry about spilling wine all over her….but I couldn't help myself!*

Tess > *I thought it was funny!* ☺

MindFreak > ☺

MindFreak > *glad ur not mad*

Tess > *like I said…she deserved it*

MindFreak > yeah…she did ☺

Tess > *ur mom is so cool!*

MindFreak > *sometimes*

Tess > *ur so lucky…wish my mom was like her*

Tess > *please say sorry to ur mom for me. I was really embarrassed*

MindFreak > *don't be embarrassed! I'm used to that…we had ron living with us, rmbr?*

Tess > *that would've been so bad*

MindFreak > *it was the worst!!*

Tess > *gotta go…my mom again*

MindFreak > *cya tmrw?*

Tess > *ok… there's something I need to tell u…cya tmrw* ☺

MindFreak > ☺

And with that, I logged off messenger and stared through my open window into the darkness of the night.

Tess wanted to hang out the following day. She had something to tell me. I could feel my curiosity taking over, and I wondered what it was. But as long as I had a chance to hang out with her, that was all that mattered.

I had no idea what was so important, but I really should have anticipated what it was. It was to be expected really, and I soon realized that if I was going to let loose with my powers, then I'd have to suffer the consequences. Whatever they were.

I just hadn't counted on what was ahead.

Tess...

When I made my way along the track towards Sam's house, I thought about how I would tell him what I'd heard the day before. Tahlia had called me with the news. And as I pushed the overgrown tree branches aside to allow me to pass through, I recalled her words vividly.

"Hey Tess, I'm just ringing to warn you about the weird kid you've hanging out with lately."

I didn't respond to that comment, instead, I rolled my eyes and waited for her to continue.

"Apparently he was the reason Jake disappeared from the disco so early last night."

As soon as the words sounded through the speaker of my phone, I felt a tingle of fear work its way down my spine.

"He's telling everyone that Sam Worthington attacked him in the sports shed. Can you believe it?"

That was when I finally responded, "Oh my gosh! Who told you that?"

"Josh Hartley told Samantha and Samantha just told me!"

"You're kidding me! Is that what Jake is telling everyone?" I could feel my heart hammering wildly in my chest as I took in the news.
"Yeah, Jake was pretty shaken up and that's why he left in such a hurry. No one knew what was wrong with him, but he told Josh all about it today. Jake says that Sam

Worthington is dangerous. And I know you've been hanging out with Sam, so I thought you should know."

Her voice had a concerned edge to it, but then I heard her laugh. "It's a pretty crazy story though. I mean, can you imagine Sam Worthington beating up Jake? It's kind of hard to believe!"

Grasping at the doubt that had crept into her voice, I focused on that argument. "That's a pretty ridiculous story, Tahlia. Seriously…Jake is twice the size of Sam!"

"Yeah," she laughed. "You're probably right! Samantha is convinced that it's true. But then, I guess it's hard to know with Jake. Maybe someone else beat him up and he's trying to blame Sam. Jake's always picking on him at school. But who knows. I guess we'll find out more on Monday."

"Okay…well thanks for letting me know, Tahlia," I replied quietly, keen to end the call.

"All good. And anyway, Tess, I really don't know why you're so interested in Sam. I admit that he's good looking in an unusual kind of way, but he's so weird! Seriously…what do you even talk about?"

Sighing into the phone, I couldn't even be bothered trying to explain. It was pointless where Tahlia and the other girls were concerned. So instead of trying, I pretended that my mom was calling me and I had to go.

"See you on Monday, Tahlia."

"See ya, Tess."
And with that, I hung up. If she knew that Sam and his mom had been invited to my house for dinner, I could only

imagine her reaction. But I'd already decided I didn't care what Tahlia, or Samantha, or the other girls thought. I could choose my own friends and as far as I was concerned, Sam was the person I wanted to hang out with most.

I wasn't sure how he would take this news, however, and when I made my way into his backyard and caught sight of him at his bedroom window, I felt my heart skip a beat.

At the same instant, he looked down towards me and I watched the wide smile light up his face completely. Aware of the familiar flutter of my heart, the same sensation that I always felt when he smiled at me that way, I waved eagerly in response.

Sam...

As soon as I spotted her through my window, I felt a shiver of excitement. It was a strange feeling, one I'd never felt before meeting Tess. And the glow of her long golden hair in the morning sunlight, made her seem almost angel-like in appearance. It seemed weird to be thinking that way, but I couldn't help it. I tried to shake the thoughts and feelings aside, but for some reason, they persisted, and there seemed nothing I could do about it.

Racing down the stairs two at a time, I headed for the front door and pulled it open wide just as she reached the top step.

"Hey!" I said, trying to rid myself of the awkward red flush I could feel creeping over my skin.

She had the strangest effect on me and I gulped nervously, not wanting to appear the weird kid that so many others made me out to be. "Come on in!"

Smiling back, she moved through the doorway and followed me to the kitchen. My mom had left earlier and wouldn't be back until later in the day, so it was a great chance for us to hang out with having Mom around.

I knew my mother tried to eavesdrop on our conversations. She pretended she didn't, but I knew she did her best to listen in on every word. Especially now she knew Tess was aware of my secret. That fact alone made Mom extra cautious about what I was saying.

The good thing was that she'd commented on what a nice

girl Tess was, and I knew she was over the moon that I finally had a friend to hang out with. But regardless of that, she was still anxious about our friendship.

"Sam, you can't be too careful!" She'd repeated these words several times and was constantly reminding me.

"I know, Mom, but stop worrying. It's okay, Tess will never tell anyone!" She had frowned at my response, and I knew she wasn't completely convinced.

With a loud sigh and a shake of her head, she continued, "And I don't want to see you pulling another stunt like you did last night! That wine glass was nowhere near Janice's hand at the time, it was impossible for her to have knocked it over. I knew straight away it was you!"

I grinned at her, "Yeah, but she didn't realize that. And you've gotta admit it was pretty funny! The look on her face was priceless!"

"Plus she deserved it!" I added with a smirk. "You have to agree with me on that one!"

Mom laughed at the memory. "Yes, ok, she did deserve it, and I do admit that it actually was quite hilarious. I was struggling to keep a straight face! I have no idea how Tess and John put up with her though! She's not the easiest person to get along with, that's for sure!"

"You've got that right!" I nodded in agreement. "Tess's dad is cool, but I don't like her mom. When I first met her she seemed really friendly and nice, just like Tess. But she's nothing like Tess at all. What she was saying about you...it made me so angry!"

"Oh, I'm used to narrow minded people like her, Sam. You

know that. There will always be the haters and the critics. If they don't understand something, they can't accept it. It's just the way people are. They're just not worth worrying about."

As an afterthought, she continued, her tone becoming more serious, "Just promise me you'll be careful!"

"I promise, Mom," I replied solemnly, and then on a whim, I gave her a quick hug before heading back up to my room. "See you when you get back."

She looked at me in surprise as she watched me walk away. "See you later Sam. I'll be back late this afternoon."

I knew it was unusual for me to show much affection around my mom. Hugging her just wasn't my thing. And every time she tried to grab hold of me, I shrugged away. But after seeing Tess's mom in action, I'd suddenly come to appreciate my own mother a lot more. I knew she enjoyed the occasional hug, it was the least I could do to show her I really did care. She was strange and a little weird in her own way, but she was still my mom, and she was the only one who really understood me.

But that morning when I looked at Tess, who was perched on a stool at our kitchen bench top, I was glad Mom wasn't around. It was nice to talk to Tess without worrying about my mother overhearing our conversation. While Mom appeared to be chilled out and easy-going, deep inside, I knew she worried a lot.

Her concerns were mainly about me and my powers. That was what bothered her most. Her constant fear of someone finding out and sweeping me away into some sort of research facility for experimentation and tests was her biggest nightmare. I knew it was something that remained constant in her mind and she continued to remind me of that fact.

But the sight of Tess's smiling face that morning, pushed all other thoughts aside. I watched her as she sipped from the glass of freshly squeezed juice left from breakfast that morning, and when I offered her one of Mom's home-baked muffins, her face lit up with delight. They were freshly baked and the beautiful aroma still wafted around the kitchen.

"Oh my gosh, yes please!" Tess exclaimed as she eyed the tray of warm muffins in front of her. "Your mom's cooking is the best!"

When she bit into the soft and doughy center of the muffin, pieces of cooked apple poked out from the interior, and I could see the pleasure clearly marked on Tess's features.

"Oh my gosh," she repeated again, "these are delicious!"

We sat in comfortable silence as we munched away, enjoying the taste sensation in front of us. And then with a huge grin, she mentioned the incident at dinner the evening before. "I still can't believe you spilled wine all over my mom!"

Tess's expression was filled with amusement, and within seconds we were both in fits of laughter over her mother's surprised reaction.

"She had no idea!" Tess giggled. "Her expression was the best. I was in shock myself at first. I was seriously thinking, OMG, Mom, you are so embarrassing! But then I realized you'd caused it, and I almost burst out laughing. I know I shouldn't say this, but it was so funny."

"Yeah, it was pretty funny," I nodded. "But, like I said last night, I couldn't help myself."

She stared at me for a moment, taking in my words. But then all of a sudden, her smile abruptly faded away. "There's something I have to tell you!"

I stared back at her, a sinking feeling creeping into my stomach.

Sighing heavily, her face filled with despair, "I didn't get a chance to say anything last night, but Tahlia called me yesterday. And apparently Jake is telling everyone that you attacked him!"
I sat grim-faced and silent. What could I say? Jake was telling the truth. Even though I hadn't attacked him with my fists or any parts of my physical body, whether he deserved it or not, I had still attacked him. And I knew there would have to be repercussions of some sort. That had been in the back of my mind ever since it had all happened.

However, I was kind of prepared.

"Who's going to believe him?" I asked.

I looked at Tess, trying to gauge her reaction to my logical explanation. "As if anyone would believe that I beat up Jake Collins!"

I paused for effect, waiting for her to comprehend what I was saying. "I'm the weirdo loser kid that he picks on every day; the weakling who doesn't have the guts to retaliate. Remember?"

"Plus, he's twice the size of me!"

"And besides that," I continued in a rush, "there isn't a mark on him because I never touched him! If he was bruised and battered, then he might have an argument. But there's no evidence at all."

Tess stared back at me, processing my words. Her mind seemed to tick over as she took everything in.

"What about the sports shed? It looks like it had a cyclone rip through it! That's pretty good evidence, wouldn't you agree?" she reminded me of the one obvious fact that she thought I was clearly missing.
"Yeah, it is," I admitted with a nod. "But I've already thought about that. And I have the perfect solution!"

Pausing once again, I raised my eyebrows and spoke, not completely sure how she would react to what I had to say. But I had decided to say it anyway. "We can sneak into the school grounds today and get it all cleaned up!"

She stared back at me incredulously. "What??? Are you serious?? Aren't you in enough trouble as it is? Now you want to get caught for trespassing as well? If someone sees us, we'll both be in more trouble than ever!"

"Well…we just have to make sure we don't get caught!" I grinned back at her.

She shook her head in disbelief. Clearly, my idea was the most absurd thing she had ever heard. "But the shed will probably be locked. Surely the hall and all the other buildings would've been locked after the disco.'

"A little padlock won't stop me!" I grinned.

She frowned back at me, her mouth agape, and I could see her attempting to comprehend my words.

"Of course, you don't have to come with me, Tess," I added earnestly. "This is my mess and I can sort it out on my own. I don't want you getting into trouble over this!"

I waited for a moment before continuing. "But I could sure use a little help!"

Tess…

I couldn't believe what Sam was suggesting! To break into the school sports shed on a Sunday afternoon and try to clean up the mess, was such a crazy idea!

But after my initial shock, the idea began to take hold and work its way through my mind. As ridiculous as it had first sounded, all it took was a few seconds to think it over and I found myself nodding in agreement.

"I can't believe I'm saying this, but…what's your plan?"

I stared back at Sam, the sight of his confident grin removing any doubt from my mind. Even though I knew I was taking a risk, I felt safe with him, and I was convinced that he would never intentionally cause me harm or danger.

The fact that we could get caught was definitely a worry, but I had faith in what he was suggesting. And when we headed out the door and made our way along the track through to my front garden, I could feel my pulse racing with excitement.

Before meeting him, my life had been a boring existence. The most exciting thing I ever did was hang out at the mall with my best friend, Casey and see an occasional movie. Her parents weren't as strict as mine and she had a lot more freedom, but my freedom was extremely limited.
School work and grades were what was most important in my mother's mind. Projects, homework, and reading were what she preferred to see me doing in my spare time. Unless I had a book of some kind in my hand, she accused me of wasting time.

The trick now was to convince her to let me go for a bike ride with Sam. Surely there was no harm in that!

We headed along the track towards my house, Sam wheeling his bike beside him. And when we reached the open grass area of the front yard, I realized that luck was on our side.

My mother's car was nowhere to be seen. When I left for Sam's house an hour earlier, her car had been parked in full view in our driveway. But it had since disappeared, which could only mean one thing.

On Sunday mornings, she usually visited the local farmer's market to buy fresh fruit and vegetables for the week. The market was only held on Sundays and she had recently started shopping there, deciding they had fresher produce and cheaper prices than the supermarkets. That had to be the reason her car was missing and she was nowhere in sight.

Then I spotted my dad, who was making his way from the back of the house with the lawnmower. I smiled at him sweetly. "Dad, is it okay if I go for a bike ride with Sam? There's some cool bike paths in our neighborhood that he wants to show me. It's too nice a day to stay indoors."

I looked at Dad innocently while I waited for him to switch off the noisy lawn mower so he could hear me properly. After repeating my request one more time, he glanced from me to Sam.

"Hello, Mr. Hawkins," Sam smiled politely. "It's such a great day for a ride and I thought I could show Tess around the neighborhood. The tracks start just down the street from here and there's a really nice path we can follow that leads along the lake."

Dad paused to think for a moment before responding, "Well, it is a beautiful day, and it would be nice to see you kids enjoying it. How long do you plan to head out for?"

"Oh, probably for a few hours," Sam replied. "It's quite a long track and we may as well make the most of the day."

"Well, that sounds fine to me," Dad nodded again, "Just take your phone with you, Tess, in case your mom wants you back home for some reason."

"Sure dad," I grinned, and giving him a quick hug, I hurried into the house to grab my phone before he could change his mind.

After searching the garage for my bike and helmet, I followed Sam down the street, while at the same time, the thumping beat of my heart pounded in my chest. I knew it wasn't from the effort of trying to keep up with Sam. We were riding at a steady pace and it was really no effort at all. My racing heartbeat was related to something completely different.

As if in sync with what I was feeling, Sam turned briefly back towards me, and grinning widely in return, I took in the beaming smile on his face.

Sam...

My head was in a whirl of excitement as I pedaled along the track. Even though my plan was a little risky, Tess had agreed to come along and that was what mattered most.

I had never known what it was like to have a best friend of my own. Sure, I had my online gamer friends, but that was completely different. And there were the few guys that I sometimes hung out with at school. But most of the time I was on my own.

Nothing had ever come close to the feeling of having a friend who I could trust and rely on. The fact that Tess was a girl didn't matter. She was genuinely happy to hang out with me, and it was the best feeling in the entire world.

As excited as I was, I had no idea of the dangers that lay ahead. That was something I was yet to find out, and I would also learn that Tess's loyalty would be tested.

But right then I was oblivious to that fact, and I cycled along the track with my pulse racing and Tess pedaling along behind me.

Tess...

When we reached the main school building, we headed past the front entrance towards the back, in the hope of not being seen.

I knew that a lot of kids cut through the school grounds as a short-cut on their way to the other side of town. And I figured that if anyone did happen to spot us, we could say that was what we were doing.

As we had to pass the sports shed on our way, it was a logical route to take. Sam's plan was for me to hide behind the nearby clump of bushes that bordered the fence line behind the rear of the shed. It was a good place to hide our bikes at least, and although I had objected as I wanted to help with the clean-up, Sam insisted that was too dangerous. If anyone was caught, he wanted it to be him alone. And besides that, it made sense for me to keep a look-out, just in case anyone happened to be walking by.

I had to admit that the plan did make sense. Added to that, Sam had a better idea of the layout of the sports shed and where all the equipment belonged. During sports sessions, Mr. Dawson had often called upon him and a couple of other kids to gather together the equipment needed for the lessons. And as Sam reminded me, he had a pretty good memory.

"It's weird, but my memory is almost photographic," he told me on one occasion when we'd been discussing his powers.

"I guess it has something to do with the telekinesis, but I can remember things so easily. It's like a picture in my mind that stays there forever!"

I tried to argue that it would be quicker if I helped him, but he wouldn't listen and insisted that I remain hidden. So we continued on our way past the sports shed door, towards the bushy tree-lined area where I was to hide with our bikes.

Glancing at the door as we made our way quickly past, my eyes fell on the heavy padlock that hung from the latch. While I assumed the door would be locked, I wasn't expecting something so solid and secure. This was something that had not been there on Friday night at the disco and I gasped in surprise.

"Oh no! It's padlocked!"

This had obviously been put in place after the disco ended and was more than likely something that the janitor had done after everyone left. I wondered for a moment if he'd thought to check inside the shed. If he had, he would have spotted the chaos straight away.

Brushing that worry aside, I focused on the lock in front of me. "That padlock looks pretty strong!" I said to Sam with a frown.

With a sly grin, he turned towards the shed door and I watched in fascination as the lock suddenly fell open and hung loosely on the latch. It was like something I'd expect to see in a Harry Potter movie where Hermione or some other witch casts a spell, causing the lock in front of her to magically open wide.

But it wasn't a movie scene and there was no Hermione, nor any other Harry Potter wizards or witches in our midst. Instead, it was just me, with my mouth open wide in surprise, and Sam grinning proudly beside me.

"OMG!" I looked at him incredulously. "You are amazing!! How on earth did you do that??"

"It's easy," he boasted. "All I have to do is see the inside of the lock in my mind and picture it turning so that the mechanism releases…just like turning a key."

"Wow!" I shook my head in awe at what I'd just witnessed. I was really impressed that he'd managed to open the lock so simply and easily.

"Well, I guess you'd better get in there," I suggested, glancing quickly around to make sure we were still alone.

Thankfully, the place appeared deserted, so it seemed we should be safe. Or so I hoped. Hurrying towards the clump of nearby trees, I pushed our bikes out of sight and crouched down low behind them.

My pulse raced anxiously as I waited for Sam to finish. Unfortunately, though, patience was not my strong point and after a few minutes, I became agitated and nervous. I knew he hadn't been in the shed long, but I was desperate for him to hurry so we could get out of there.

If my parents had any idea of what I was doing right then, I'd be grounded for life. My mother would probably lock me in my room and throw away the key. Dreading the thought of being caught out, I stood up impatiently and raced towards the shed door.

Sam...

When I heard the door creak open behind me, I whipped around to face it. I didn't dare breathe as I moved quickly behind a tall shelf of equipment in an attempt to hide.

The shed was shrouded in semi-darkness as I hadn't dared to switch on the light. But there was a small window on the rear wall that was partly covered by a tall cupboard, and it allowed enough light to be able to see.

Peering carefully through a gap in the shelving, I saw a strong shaft of sunlight filter through as the door was quickly pushed open. However, I didn't catch a glimpse of whoever had entered, before the door was abruptly closed behind them.

"Sam! Sam, where are you?" The distinct sound of Tess's voice carried through the semi-darkness, and I breathed a huge sigh of relief.

"You're supposed to be keeping watch outside!" Stepping out from my hiding spot, I stared towards her. "That was our agreement, remember?"

"I know. I'm sorry," she apologized. "But you were taking so long! I thought I should come and help!"

I couldn't resist laughing at her comment. It was such a gross exaggeration as I'd only been in the shed for a few minutes. But now that she was there, I figured she may as well stay to help.

"Alright then," I grinned, "if you really want to help, how

about you start with all the balls. The basketballs go in that tub in the corner and the smaller ones belong in the basket. I'll get everything else sorted."

And focusing on the layer of baseball bats that were lying in an untidy heap, I lifted them into the air and watched them zip across the shed onto the shelf where they belonged. All I had to do was straighten the pile, to try and make them as neat as possible.

Tess laughed in amusement and I turned to look at her in the semi-darkness behind me, "That is so cool! I didn't even think of you using your powers to get this mess sorted out!"

I grinned back at her, but just as I turned to pick up a couple of javelin spears, I heard the sound of approaching voices that appeared to be getting louder by the second.

Instantly realizing that some kids were making their way past the shed, I froze in my spot, at the same time putting a finger to my lips warning Tess to stay quiet. The only thing I could hear right then, apart from the approaching voices, was the hammering thump of my heart.

Tess...

I stared back at Sam, who was standing stock still on the opposite side of the semi-darkened shed. My breath was caught in my throat as the approaching voices gradually became louder.

Within seconds, we could hear them right outside the shed door, and I prayed for whoever was there to keep walking. Our original plan had been for me to throw a pebble at the rear wall of the shed, to alert Sam if I noticed anyone heading in that direction. From my spot in the nearby bushes I had a good vantage point and a clear view of the area.

In theory, I should have had ample time to warn him. But we quickly realized that even the best plans don't always go the way they were intended. And in this particular case, I'd completely changed our plan anyway.

Suddenly the loud voice of a kid sounded just outside the shed door. "Hey, looks like someone has left the sports shed unlocked."

Over the pounding beat of my heart, I heard another kid say, "Do you wanna check it out? I could use a new basketball. Mine keeps going flat on me, I think it must have a slow leak."

The first kid seemed hesitant, and I held my breath as I waited for his response. "Yeah, I guess we could. But everything's labeled with the school name, isn't it? If your mom or anyone else sees that, you'll be busted for sure."

"Yeah, I guess you're right. Let's not worry about it. Hopefully, I'll get a new one for my birthday anyway."

Just as I breathed a sigh of relief, I heard the pinging sound of a text on my phone. The loud noise burst into the silence surrounding us, and I gasped with fright.

Shoving my hand deep into my back pocket, I tried to wrench my phone free, desperate to reach it before it sounded again. My phone had a double alert signal and if a text wasn't responded to within a few seconds, a second alert tone sounded.

Frantic to pull it free I tugged wildly at my pocket, cursing my decision to wear that particular pair of shorts. They had such tiny pockets and it was always an effort to remove anything from them.

My phone seemed caught on some stitching or something and I struggled to grasp a proper hold of it. With my mind racing anxiously, I finally managed to pull it out. But in my haste, I fumbled clumsily with it as I tried to prevent it from smashing onto the concrete floor at my feet.

Sam...

When I heard the loud pinging sound, I figured it must be a text or some kind of alert on Tess's phone, and I stared in horror towards her.

Placing a finger on my lips I tried to indicate for her to keep quiet but it seemed that she was preoccupied with trying to pull her phone from her pocket.

The last thing we needed was for a couple of kids to burst into the shed and find us there. And I quickly moved back out of sight into the darkened corner. At the same time, I tried to get Tess's attention to do the same thing. But her focus was on her phone and the repeated sounds it was making.

Sucking in a sharp breath, I glanced at the door that one of the kids was trying to push open. Rather than swing wide, it scraped along the concrete flooring and required a good shove before it would open properly.

Thankfully, this was enough to alert Tess who quickly moved out of sight, crouching down behind the large basket of tennis balls beside her.

A shaft of bright light filled the shed and I could see the shape of two kids silhouetted against it. I had no idea who they were and didn't dare try to get a better look. All I could do was stay fixed in place. Holding my breath, I remained silent and still in the hope that they wouldn't bother to look around. Because if they did, we'd both be found for sure.

"That's weird," said one of the intruders. "I could have

sworn I heard a noise in here. It sounded like someone's phone."

"Yeah, maybe," said the other boy, "But there's no one in here, Rich. We should go before someone sees us. If Mr. Dawson finds out we've been in his shed, we'll be dead meat on Monday."

"Okay," the first kid agreed, as he turned towards the door.

And then, dragging the door closed behind them, the pair left as quickly as they had entered.

Just when I thought we were safe, I heard their voices again. "Hey, Rich, maybe we should lock the door?"

"Yeah, whatever!" Rich replied, "But hurry up. I've gotta get home!"

And with the sound of the padlock clicking into place, the boys' voices faded away into the distance.

Tess...

"Oh my gosh, that was so close!" I whispered to Sam as I got to my feet. "And they've locked the door! Lucky, you have your powers or we'd be stuck in here all night!"

"That's just it," Sam replied, the concern sounding in his voice. "The padlock is on the other side of the door. I'm not sure if I can do anything without having it in view."

"What?" I gasped. "You've got to be kidding me! Do you mean that you can't open it?"

I raised my arms in despair and ran my fingers through my hair, pushing it anxiously out of my face. This plan was definitely not turning out the way it was supposed to, and I blamed myself for not doing as Sam had asked.

"This is a disaster!" I exclaimed, "And it's all my fault!"

"No, it's not," Sam said, a hint of frustration in his own voice. "I'm the one to blame. I caused all this in the first place. If I hadn't lost my temper so badly, neither of us would be here right now!"

I stopped for a moment to breathe. There had to be an answer.

"Sam," I said, moving closer towards him. "How do you know you can't open that lock? I've seen you do incredible things. You even made a tree branch fall from a tree! If you can do that, then I'm sure you can open that lock. You just have to believe in yourself. Sam, I know you can do it!"

He stared at me then, and even in the dim light of the shed, I could see the anger in his expression. But I knew it wasn't directed at me. It was there because of his own inner frustration. I understood it clearly. And instinctively I knew that he just had to channel that anger. That was the answer. I was sure of it.

Grabbing him by the hand, I pulled him gently towards the door.

"Picture that padlock in your mind, Sam. Focus on it. Pretend that it's Jake Collins who's threatening you, instead of a silly padlock. You can do it, Sam, you just have to put your mind to it!"

I stood silently by and watched. With the light that shone from beneath the door, I had a reasonable view of his face and I could see his eyes begin to glaze over. Filled with deep concentration, he stared towards the door in the very spot where the latch was fixed to the other side.

Seconds later, I heard what sounded like a faint click. Then another click could be heard, but that time it was louder. After that, the sound of the door latch as it scraped across the metal surface of the shed was unmistakable.

Pulling firmly on the door, I managed to yank it open and the pavement and nearby buildings came into full view.

"Oh my gosh, you did it!!" I struggled to keep my voice down as I threw my arms around Sam's neck in a grateful hug.

It was spontaneous and unplanned. I didn't even think about what I was doing, my relief was so immense. To me right then, Sam was a hero. But I caught his awkward and shy expression, and feeling slightly awkward myself, I moved my hands away.

Glancing behind me, I realized there were still some remaining pieces of equipment scattered on the floor. As quickly as I could, I gathered everything together then shoved it all onto the nearest shelves. At that moment, I didn't care whether it was packed away properly or not. My priority was for us both to get out of there and as far away as quickly as possible.

Meanwhile, Sam remained slightly dazed in his spot by the door. So I grasped hold of his hand and pulled him outside, pushing the door closed behind us. After yanking the latch in place and tightly securing the padlock, I led him towards the clump of trees where our bikes were still camouflaged by the surrounding bush.

It wasn't until we were completely free of the school grounds and pedaling along a nearby bike track that I finally breathed a sigh of relief. And when I turned quickly to check on Sam who was cycling along behind me, I raised one arm in the air in jubilation.

"We did it, Sam! We did it!"

Sam...

As I rode along, I concentrated on the girl ahead of me. Her long blond hair flowed in waves down her back, and the pedals of her bike turned in a fluid motion as she cycled along the track. She was the coolest person I had ever met. And when she turned and whooped in the air at our success, I felt my heart leap with joy.

A happiness that I'd never known before settled over me. I finally had a best friend and I vowed I would do anything I could to protect her.

That afternoon she had been a hero, but I never wanted to put her in danger again. I felt a responsibility that I'd never felt before and I welcomed the tingling feeling it gave me.

For once I felt appreciated and wanted. I was no longer some hopeless, loser, weirdo freak that very few people wanted anything to do with. Instead, I had the coolest girl in the world as my friend, and I was filled with pride.

However, I was not prepared to be trampled back down once more. After feeling so powerful and strong, I did not think it could ever be possible.

But I hadn't counted on Jake's persistence nor the revenge that he was determined he deserved.

That was not something I expected at all.
And neither of us ever expected to bump into him that afternoon. But when we did, I knew immediately that we were in trouble.

Tess...

The track that led along the edge of the lake was everything that Sam had promised. It was a beautiful sunny afternoon and the water sparkled invitingly. It appeared to be a great spot for a picnic or a swim during the summer months, and I imagined how popular it must be for local kids and families. Taking in the beauty of the area, one that I hadn't realized existed so close to home, I looked forward to the warmer part of the year when I could enjoy it further.

We passed by one lone rider who smiled to us as he pedaled by.

But apart from him, the bike path which doubled as a walking track was deserted. All I could hear was the whirring of our bike pedals and the crunch of the gravel beneath us. A feeling of satisfaction settled over me. As well as that, a sense of pride for being able to help Sam. Although we were almost caught out, it had all ended well, and the thrill was like nothing I'd ever experienced before.
When we came to the section where the track widened, I

slowed down so Sam could ride alongside me. As we pedaled, we chatted and laughed about our daring adventure. Still caught up in the excitement, it was the only thing we could think of or talk about.

When we rounded a bend in the pathway, I noticed an open grassy area ahead. It looked to be a lovely picnic spot and I imagined the fun we could have there during the summer. But as we neared the clearing, a figure abruptly appeared on the track. Where he had come from, I had no idea, and my pulse immediately quickened.

The chances of bumping into him right then were so remote. And the breath caught in my throat as I glanced nervously towards Sam.

Sam…

As soon as I saw Jake standing there, an inner intuition told me that we were in trouble. Tess and I were alone on that track. Apart from one lone bike rider who was long gone, we hadn't passed another soul. And when a group of kids appeared on the pathway alongside Jake, I felt a gut-wrenching fear take hold.

"What the heck is he doing here?" I murmured to Tess, as I pulled to a halt a short distance back from the group.

Jake and his friends were blocking our path and our choice was to turn back or to try and ride around them. Glancing towards the large patch of open grass at their side, I spotted their bikes sprawled haphazardly over the area and a row of fishing rods set up on a small jetty that jutted out over the water. The rods were leaning against the handrails with their attached lines cast out into the water below.

Without a heap of swimmers disturbing the water, I'd heard that the lake was a great place to fish. But whether Jake and his friends had managed to catch anything that day, was the furthest thing from my mind. My only concern was getting Tess safely home, and avoiding the drama that I pictured unfolding in front of me.

Sometimes I had visions, and scenes would play on my mind, almost like pressing the 'Play' button for a movie. Except in my case, it was real-life experiences that I saw in my head. It didn't happen often and usually, there would only be flashes of faces and incidents. The problem was, these flashes always occurred just moments before the real-life events took place.

When I asked my mom about it, she said it sounded similar to what she saw in her mind as well, and that I had clearly inherited some of her psychic abilities. While some people might think this would be a cool trait to have, I felt the opposite. I had enough weird stuff going on in my head, without adding psychic abilities to my growing list of unusual skills. And besides, what use was being psychic when I was barely given any warning.

My mom could see things far into the future, and tell people in detail what lay ahead for them, months or even years down the track. But for me, it was just brief flashes, like a sudden signal, warning me of something that was about to occur; the warning appearing in my mind just minutes or even seconds before the event took place in real life.

And what I was picturing in my head right then, was not good.

It was not good at all.

In an attempt to muster the inner confidence that had been with me earlier, I hopped off my bike, wheeled it in front of Tess like a protective barrier, and stood my ground.

Focusing on calming my breathing as well as the rapid racing of my pulse, I glared at the group in front of me. And all the while, I remained aware of my primary goal…to protect the one important person in my life right then.

Apart from my mom, Tess was the only real friend I had, and I was not going to let anything happen to her.

Tess...

In that instant, as I stood behind Sam and stared towards Jake and his group of friends, something abruptly occurred to me. It was a strange thought to be having in that moment. But I realized that ever since meeting Sam, my life had become like a very tense roller coaster ride, full of unexpected anxious events occurring one after the other.

Tahlia's words on the phone rang once more in my ears...*I just wanted to warn you about that weird kid you've been hanging out with lately...*

And then my mom's voice sounded loud and clear as well...*I'm not sure about you spending so much time with that boy. Something about him seems a bit odd. I can't put my finger on it, I'm just not sure what it is...*

They had been my mother's words just that morning when I asked for permission to head to Sam's house. She frowned and shook her head. And for a moment, I thought she was going to say no.

I hadn't bothered replying to her comment. If I had, we would have ended up in an argument for sure. Instead, I told her I wouldn't be gone long and then I'd left. Luckily, while I was gone, she left for the fruit and vegetable market. But I also realized, that if she had remained at home and prevented my bike ride with Sam, I wouldn't have found myself confronted by Jake and all his followers.

Try as I might to push those thoughts aside, I could not help the chill of alarm that was causing goose bumps to appear on my skin. Even though it was a warm day and the sun was shining brightly, a cold sensation was working its way up my spine.

Rather than the fear that I had expected to see on Jake's face after the incident in the sports shed, he seemed filled with an inner rage, and the look of anger on his face was too real to ignore.

Sam...

"What are the chances of seeing you here today?" Jake smirked at me, a confident grin on his face.

I hadn't previously anticipated that reaction at all. Definitely not after what had happened in the sports shed. Jake was supposed to be scared of *me* now! Everything should have changed and our roles should have been reversed. But it was quite clear that the scenario I faced right then, was not what I'd hoped for. He had his gang of followers to back him up and had returned to the old Jake who strutted around thinking he was better than everyone else and that no one could stop him.

"I was telling the boys about your magic tricks." His face turned to a snarl as he spat the words, "I've gotta admit the stunt you pulled the other night was pretty impressive. But you don't fool me! You're just a weirdo freak with a psychic nutcase for a mother. And I don't appreciate your stupid stunt."

He paused for a moment to allow his words to take effect. And then he continued. "No one does something like that to me and gets away with it."

I could tell he was waiting for a reaction. He was trying to get me to retaliate. Anything to give him an excuse to beat me up. He knew he was physically more powerful, plus he had his gang of supporters behind him. It would be an easy fight – all of them against me. I was convinced that was what he had in mind.

He was too stupid to even consider that I could repeat my

"magic act" once more. With the support of his friends, he thought he was invincible and had nothing to worry about. I guessed that was how bullies operated. Their groups of followers were what gave them power. It was all becoming quite clear to me, and I filed that information away for future reference as I continued to stand my ground.

And even though I could feel the anger bubbling inside me, I forced myself to remain calm as I stared back at him quietly, refusing to say a word.

Walking closer towards me, he pulled himself up tall, his huge body size shadowing mine. "So, weirdo freak. You don't expect me to let you get away with what you did. Do you?"

When I still didn't respond, he had no choice but to keep taunting, and with a rough poke of his finger on my chest, he shoved me slightly backward. "Say something! You freak!!"

Sucking in a rush of air, I tried to stand tall, to prove to him that I wasn't afraid. I knew he was looking for fear in my eyes. That was what he fed on, just like any predator would do. But if I stood up to him, perhaps he would back down and leave me alone. That was what I hoped.

But I should have guessed it wouldn't work that way. He was obviously intent on revenge and wouldn't be satisfied until he got it. And like a pack of hungry wolves, his buddies took a step forward, each of them as threatening as Jake. I knew that I had no time to waste and that one way or another I had to do something.

But my mother's words of warning sounded for the umpteenth time in my head....*Sam, promise me you'll be careful. If anyone else finds out about your powers, that'll be the end for us. Just remember to breathe Sam. Breathe and stay in control. That's all you have to do...stay in control.*

Taking another deep breath, I glared at the threatening figure in front of me.

Tess...

Jake and his friends were such jerks. And in that instant, I felt disgusted at the thought of everyone turning a blind eye and letting them get away with how they behaved. It was wrong.

On impulse, I jumped to Sam's defense.

My heart racing, I stared defiantly at Jake. "Just back off, Jake. Seriously, what is your problem?"

He looked at Sam shaking his head in disgust. "You're such a loser! You need a girl to defend you. Ha Ha! What a joke!"

He turned to his friends with a smirk. He was not going to let it go, I could see that quite clearly.

But I didn't know what to do. I was so scared that Sam would let loose the way he had in the sports shed, and then something really terrible would happen. I was sure Sam could not take too much more of Jake's torment, and he would be forced to put him in his place once and for all.

I looked anxiously at Sam, a feeling of panic creeping into my stomach. Catching the familiar dazed look in his eyes, I felt an instant prickle on my skin. Shaking my head nervously, I willed him not to react.

Without any warning, a loud rustle sounded in the trees around us. Previously there had not been a breath of wind. But a strong breeze had whipped up out of nowhere and was making an eerie whistling sound as it passed through the surrounding shrubs and tree branches.
But it was the sudden scraping sound that caught everyone's attention. And we each turned towards the jetty, where the fishing rods that had been left leaning against the handrails were being blown around by the strong breeze.

I looked back at Sam, wondering if he was somehow responsible for the abrupt change in the weather. The angry expression remained on his face but he did not say a word.

"The rods!" one of the boys yelled, an edge of panic in his voice as he raced towards the jetty.

The other boys ran after him, each of them realizing their precious rods were in danger of falling into the water. Jake remained fixed in his spot. "Hey guys, can you grab mine as well!"

In typical Jake style, he simply stood by and watched, as his friends ran in a frenzied rush to save their rods from disappearing into the deep waters of the lake. Before they could reach the jetty, however, one of the rods fell down onto the timber decking and was blown forcefully along the rough surface. Realizing that it was his rod at risk, Jake sprang into action to save it.

Watching the scene unfold, I smiled with satisfaction as the rod continued its journey along the length of the jetty, with Jake running after it. The sight was so comical, I could not help but laugh. And when I caught the grin on Sam's face as well, I shook my head at him in awe.

I wasn't surprised when the rod blew right off the end and out of view. That was when we hopped onto our bikes and quickly cycled away. I doubted that Jake would ever see that particular fishing rod again, and as I pedaled quickly along behind Sam, I decided that Jake deserved everything he got.

Sam's idea was ingenious! Apart from Jake losing his fishing rod, no harm had been done and no one had been hurt. "Distracting them like that was so clever, Sam!" I cycled alongside him, my pulse still racing furiously over what had just happened.

"Yeah! I thought so too!" he grinned proudly back. "The idea suddenly came to me, so I just went with it!"

"Seriously though, you created a really strong wind! It came up out of nowhere! Do you even realize how strong your powers are? I mean, that was incredible!! And look, it's still blowing!"

I had to push against the force of the gale that continued to howl around us, and I shook my head in wonder again. But at the same time, Sam seemed to take it all in his stride. He was so different to Jake who constantly bragged about how good he was.

It was then that I noticed the determined expression on

Sam's face. I suspected that even though he tried not to show it, there was a lot going on inside his head. I could only imagine what it must be like for him. And now he would be forced to deal with Jake the following day at school. I sighed heavily at that thought. If Jake kept pushing and tormenting Sam, surely it would eventuate in disaster. I tried not to focus on that idea, but it persisted in my mind.

But my thoughts were suddenly interrupted by the sound of a text on my phone. Slowing to a stop, I pulled my phone from my back pocket. But when I realized who the message was from, I shook my head in dismay.

Where are you?

There were three simple words and that was all. But my mother's tone registered clearly in my brain. And I could already hear her reaction when I walked in the door.

Where have you been, Tess? I told you I'm not keen on you spending too much time with that boy! And then you take off on your bike to goodness knows where! Without even a message to let us know when you'll be home!

I was prepared for the rant that was sure to come, and doing my best to avoid a huge argument, I typed a quick response.

Will be home soon!

As I cycled the rest of the way home, I was filled with an uneasy sensation about what lay ahead. I was used to my mother's rants. Admittedly they seemed to be getting worse, but it was the worry of Sam's powers that weighed on my mind. His was a crushing secret to keep, and although I would never betray him, I could not forgive myself if something terrible happened that I could have somehow helped to prevent.

As if reading my thoughts, he turned to me with a reassuring smile. I managed a small smile in return but the nervous anxiety that was overwhelming me right then remained sitting heavily in the pit of my stomach.

Sam...

When I cycled past Tess's house, I waved goodbye to her as she turned into her driveway. Catching a glimpse of her mom at the front door as I rode by, I noticed the annoyed expression on her face, and I could feel her eyes on mine as I passed. I gave her a small wave regardless and continued on my way.

I had no idea what her problem was, and I felt sorry for Tess. I just hoped that Tess didn't get into too much trouble. If she did, I was to blame. She had only gone because I'd asked her to, and I felt the guilt weigh me down. Once again, I was to blame.

When I reached my front door, I discovered that my mom wasn't home yet, so I headed to the kitchen to find something to eat. This was never a problem in my house, as Mom kept the fridge stocked with food. While the choices were limited to her home-baked recipes, I didn't complain. I was used to eating the healthy food that she cooked, and besides that, she usually made the dishes that I really enjoyed. She'd learned long ago, that I would go without, rather than eat her lentil patties, so she always made sure there was something available that I would actually eat.

As I sat at the kitchen benchtop munching on the food in front of me, I thought about Tess and what she had done for me that day. Helping me to clean up the shed and risk getting caught in the process was amazing enough. But the way she had stood up to Jake was something else.

Most kids were either in awe of him and thought he was the

coolest kid they'd ever met. Or they were simply too scared to go anywhere near him. But no one ever tried to put him in his place the way that Tess had done. Although he'd made me out to be an even bigger loser, I still appreciated her efforts. To have someone willing to stick up for me, a best friend who actually had my back, felt awesome. And while I still wasn't sure of how Tess felt about me, she was definitely the closest friend I'd ever had.

I had to admit that the idea of creating a diversion was a genius one, and I grinned proudly as I recalled the worried look on the boys' faces. Causing their precious rods to blow about in the wind was a brilliant move, and I was so glad that I'd thought of it. Although I still had no idea where the idea came from or the strength that gave me the ability to make it happen.

When I thought about it some more, I realized that what Tess had said was quite true. It would have taken a lot of ability to create that strong gale, which meant my powers must definitely be getting stronger. I also realized that I had no idea of the limits I would eventually be capable of.

The main thing was that we'd managed to get home unscathed. Apart from Jake's fishing rod disappearing into the lake, there was no other harm done. And I was sure that none of the boys suspected I had anything to do with what had happened.
But the Jake problem was obviously still a big issue. And one I would have to face the next day at school. I just wished that he'd give up and leave me alone. That was all I asked.

A picture of his face flashed into my mind and I clenched my fists angrily. Just the thought of him caused my head to overheat and I felt my face flush with frustration. Without warning, the glass of juice in front of me shattered into tiny pieces and the orange liquid spilled all over the benchtop.

But what bothered me more than the mess I had to clean up, was the thought of what I'd do to Jake if he didn't stop bugging me.

And if it came to that, he would deserve everything I gave him!

Tess...

As I stood at the bus stop waiting for the school bus to arrive, I glanced down the street towards Sam's house. He had told me on messenger the night before that he'd see me there in the morning.

Being able to message him that way, was so much fun, and I had added Casey, my best friend from my old school as well. She loved online games and I thought she'd probably enjoy the one that Sam played. Even if she didn't play the game, we could use the messenger function to chat. There were a bunch of really cool icons and effects that made it more fun than Instagram. And the best part was that my mom didn't know about it, so she wouldn't see our messages.

Mom had access to my Instagram account and often checked it. That was the only way she allowed me to set up an account in the first place. To begin with, she wouldn't permit me to have access to any social media at all. But I'd begged and begged. Nearly everyone else at my old school used Instagram. I was one of the only kids in my class who didn't have an account.

When we moved to our new house and I had to change schools, she finally agreed. Thankfully my argument about wanting to keep in touch with all my friends eventually convinced her. Ever since, Casey and I had messaged each other constantly. And without Instagram, I didn't know what we would do.

"Why can't you just call Casey on the telephone?" Mom asked me at one stage. "Isn't that the logical thing to do when you want to speak to a friend?"

I sighed in exasperation at her suggestion. She just didn't get it. And no amount of explaining would work. But in the end, she had finally given in on the condition that she had access to my username and password so she could do a regular check.

When I discovered I could message Sam via his gaming site, I decided it wouldn't hurt to have a private place to chat. It wasn't as though we were doing anything bad. All we did was talk to each other, and my conversations with him were ones that I especially did not want my mother to see.

But I wanted to include Casey more in my new life. I would never tell her about Sam's secret of course, but I was still keen to tell her about Sam himself. So far, I hadn't mentioned him at all in my Instagram messages. Mainly because I knew my mom would read them, and that was a private conversation that I really didn't want to share with her.

At least now I had a way of talking privately to Casey as well. I missed her so much. She and I had been together in the same class right from our first day at school. We were inseparable from the beginning and had shared all our secrets. Leaving her behind had been the hardest part of moving.

Although we were still close and contacted each other regularly, it wasn't the same as seeing her every day. And so far, I hadn't met any girls at school who I connected with the way I did with Casey. The only person who came close was Sam. The fact that he was a boy didn't matter. I loved the thrill of his telekinetic powers. The idea completely fascinated me. But apart from that, we just seemed to click, and I simply enjoyed hanging out with him.

As far as the girls in my group at school were concerned, Lacey was probably the nicest. At least she didn't make comments about my friendship with Sam. Not like the others did. They couldn't understand why I was even interested in him.

Lacey, however, was more of an individual and had her own opinions rather than being influenced by what everyone else said or thought. That was why I liked her so much. And I was sure that if she got to know Sam a little better then she'd enjoy hanging out with him as well.

It was then that I spotted Lacey heading towards me, as usual, a book in her hand. She was the biggest bookworm I had ever met, and she was constantly reading. Sometimes in class, she'd hide a book in her lap, so she could continue reading throughout the lesson. One time the teacher threatened to take the book from her and not give it back.

I had never met anyone who was so interested in reading, but that just added to Lacey's character. I often wondered how she had ever become friends with Samantha, Tahlia and the other girls in that group. She seemed so different to them.

It was only recently that Lacey had started catching my bus to school. The bus service that she previously used had been canceled, as there weren't enough kids using it. So she had to walk for fifteen minutes from her house to get to the nearest place where the bus would take her to school.

The only problem was that Lacey expected me to sit alongside her. Whereas beforehand, it was my opportunity to sit next to Sam. That morning though, it seemed that Sam must be running late as he had not appeared, and I worried for a moment about what might have happened to him.

But just as I grabbed a window seat and Lacey sat down alongside me, I spotted Sam through the window, racing along the pavement. With barely a second to spare, he managed to board the bus, just as it was pulling out from the curb.

From my spot near the back, I could see him scanning the bus looking for me. But I was unable to catch his eye and he sat down in a spare seat towards the front. Feeling a little disappointed, I tried to focus on Lacey's chatter.

She had put her book away and was intent on telling me all about the new outfit she'd bought the day before at the mall. She had been given a birthday voucher for one of the cool new shops that had recently opened, and she described the jeans and top that she managed to get at a discounted price. Luckily her voucher had covered the entire cost, so she was able to purchase a whole new outfit.

"You should come with me sometime, Tess. We can hang out at the mall for a few hours and I'll show you the best shops."
"That sounds like fun, Lacey," I smiled, as she continued to prattle on.

Although I really did like the sound of her idea, I couldn't stop thinking about Sam. During the bus ride, I had planned to warn him to avoid Jake at school that day. And while I knew that Sam would not be looking for trouble, I wanted to make every effort to ensure that nothing went wrong.

I could not rid myself of the unsettling feeling in my stomach. I just hoped that Sam stayed out of his way and there would be no more issues. That was what I tried to focus on.

But at the same time, I felt sure it wouldn't be quite that easy.

Sam...

I was in a deep sleep when my mom shook me awake that morning, and at first, I was unsure what was going on. But then I jolted awake, realizing that it was a school day and I had overslept.

The dream I was having was so intense that I could still see the images floating around in my head. It had seemed so real that I had to convince myself it was only a dream and nothing to worry about.

The sight of Jake and his men dressed in army camouflage gear with a rifle in his hand would not go away. While I knew it was because of the game I'd been playing the night before, instead of the animated characters on the screen, it was Jake who had appeared to gun me down. I could still feel the racing of my pulse as I tried to dive for cover.

It was at that moment my mom shook me awake and I glanced around the room, my head in a daze. The scenes had been so real and I could still hear the sound of bullets as they whipped past me at lightning speed. For a moment I wondered if it was some kind of warning about what lay ahead.

Shaking that crazy idea from my mind, I headed to the bathroom. I only had time for a thirty-second shower but I hoped it would help to wake me up properly before I had to race for the bus.

My mother would never allow me to leave the house without breakfast, and while she packed my lunch into my backpack, I grabbed some fruit from the fridge. Biting into an apple, I said a quick goodbye to her and rushed out the door.

That was when I felt the cold chill in the air, the one that I had completely forgotten was predicted. I briefly considered running back inside for a sweater. Realizing that would definitely cause me to miss the bus, I decided I'd just have to bear the brunt of the drop in temperature, as right then there was no other option.

I'd caught the end of the weather report on the television the night before. A cold front had been forecast which signaled the end to the unseasonably warm weather we'd been experiencing. Winter should have begun weeks earlier, but it had been a slow start this year.

Along with everyone else, I had not complained about the continuing warm weather. Our house, in particular, was very open and draughty, and extremely difficult to heat during the winter months. So it was never a season that I looked forward to. As well as tuning into the weather forecast though, there was something else that had immediately caught my attention.

The weatherman was talking about a strong wind that had whipped up in the local and surrounding areas just that afternoon. Apparently, some gusts had been so strong that residents complained about damage to their property. Frowning at that news, I made my way up the stairs to my room.

As I took the steps two at a time, I recalled the strong wind that had appeared out of nowhere and caused Jake and his friends to race desperately in the hope of saving their fishing gear.

That was when I wondered if the wind had been a coincidence, and a natural occurrence rather than something caused by my telekinesis. Perhaps I had nothing to do with it after all, and it was just good timing that the wind happened to whip up when it did.

But on the other hand, what if it had been me, and I actually had been responsible for the freak weather condition that had hit the local area? Shaking away the crazy notion, I opened my bedroom door and made my way to my computer desk. Surely that could not be possible. There was no way I could have created that!

But as much as I tried to convince myself, the doubt in my mind lingered for a long time.
And when I eventually turned off my light and went to bed, I still wondered if it could possibly be true.

Tess...

I was on edge when I arrived at school. Sam had hopped off the bus ahead of me and by the time I followed the long line of kids down the aisle of the bus and reached the pavement outside, he was nowhere to be seen.

I figured that he had decided to keep a low profile and head indoors quickly out of view, in case Jake suddenly happened to appear. This, of course, was a good plan, but once again, it prevented me from catching up with Sam before the bell signaled the start of class.

Spotting Tahlia and Samantha huddled in our usual spot against the building, Lacey and I made our way towards them.

"It's freezing today!" Samantha moaned as she rubbed her arms in an effort to stay warm.

Lacey was bouncing up and down on the spot. "Brrrr....I didn't bring a sweater! Let's go inside!"

Following the others, I fought against the strong wind that was howling across the front of the school. The area was like a wind tunnel and often quite breezy, but that morning, it was particularly strong.

We soon discovered that everyone else had the same idea and the school foyer and hallways were crowded with kids. Obviously, the school was not prepared for the cold snap as the heating had not yet been turned on. I even overheard one of the teachers complaining about how cold the buildings were.

Rubbing my arms for extra warmth, I was grateful that my mom reminded me to take a jacket before I left the house. At that time, the house was warm and I thought the idea a silly one, but as soon as I stepped outside, I felt the brisk drop in temperature and decided to listen to her advice.

"I wonder how Jake is today," Tahlia commented quietly, as she scanned the area looking for him.

"Yeah," Samantha replied, "But if he was beaten up maybe he won't be at school!"

"Do you honestly believe that Sam Worthington could beat up Jake Collins?" Tahlia asked, her eyebrows raised in disbelief. "I seriously cannot imagine that!"

"What happened?" Lacey asked curiously. "Did Sam Worthington beat up Jake Collins? You've got to be kidding me! When did this happen?"

At that point, I jumped in. I could see that the story would soon be all over the school if I didn't say something quickly. "That's crazy!" I said with a shake of my head. "I was riding my bike along the lake track yesterday and I saw Jake. He didn't have a mark on him. He seemed perfectly fine to me!"

"Well, that's weird!" Samantha exclaimed. "Jake told Josh that Sam attacked him."

"Maybe he was making it up!" Lacey suggested with a frown. "You know what Jake's like. And besides, he's got it in for Sam. You've seen the way he treats him!"

The sudden sound of Jake's voice made all of us jump in surprise. "Hey girls. Are you talking about me?" He grinned at each of us but his eyes remained on mine. I stared back at him uncomfortably.

"How are you today, Tess?" he asked, his smug smile still in place. "It was a surprise to see you yesterday. I didn't know you hung out at the lake!"

"It was a good day for a bike ride," I answered curtly, my expression not the least bit friendly.

Strangely enough, he didn't mention Sam at all. And I wondered what he was playing at. Was he embarrassed about what had happened and trying to keep it quiet? Or was there something else going on in his head? I really had no idea but decided it best not to say anything about what had happened on the track. I wanted to avoid drawing his attention to Sam. The less he thought of Sam, the better.

But that wish was short-lived because, at the sound of the morning bell, I spotted Sam walking past us on his way to the classroom. And unfortunately, I wasn't the only one to see him.

"Hey, loser!" Jake said loudly in his ear as he pushed his way past.

Seething inside, I caught up to Sam and whispered quietly, "Just ignore him, Sam. He's not worth it! Ignore him and he'll eventually stop!"

I gave him a reassuring smile as I made my way towards the back of the room, angrily dwelling on what Jake had just said.

With a sigh, I realized that if Jake made me so angry, he must really be having an impact on Sam. And there I was telling Sam to simply ignore him; just like the teachers continually reminded us to do if someone was bothering us. Well, that might work in some cases, but this had gone way past the ignoring stage.

Something definitely had to be done. So far nothing else had worked, and I could see that we needed help to get the situation under control. Formulating a plan in my mind, I sat down at my desk, making sure to give Jake a scathing look as I passed him.

Sam...

I tried to take on board Tess's advice. Ignoring Jake Collins, I sat at my desk and attempted to focus on the teacher's voice. But I could feel his eyes on me. The sensation of someone continually watching me was like a relentless burning that would not go away. Unable to resist a quick glance, I turned my head slightly in his direction.

That was not enough to be able to see him though, so with no other choice, I whipped my head completely around and caught his eye. Glaring back at me, he shook his head slowly. The confident grin was gone but I could see the determination in his eyes. Even from my spot across the room, it seemed to jump out at me.

Sucking in a quick breath, I returned my attention to the front of the room. Outside, the wind had become a frenzied howl, and the glass of the window beside me rattled and shook. It felt as though a hurricane was thrashing wildly around the schoolyard, and I caught sight of a metal trash can lid being blown noisily across the paved lunch area.

Grateful for the heating that had been switched on and was gradually warming the room, I looked towards our teacher who was in the process of explaining various methods of mental computation. But even though I usually liked math and was pretty good at it, I found it difficult to concentrate. Zoning out from the teacher's voice and the presence of kids around me, the sound of the wind became a distant fog in my brain. And I found my thoughts returning to the intense dream I had been woken from just a short time earlier.

Each scene played in my mind, and I remembered every

detail. I could see Jake racing towards me, his men stealthily approaching from another direction. They thought they were camouflaged by their surroundings, but I had a partial view from where I could spy on them unnoticed. It provided little shelter, however, and I knew I'd soon be spotted. So I quickly scanned the area for a better place to hide, but at the same time, my heart thumped loudly in my chest.

Boom! Boom! Boom!

Like the steady beat of a drum, it pounded; while I crouched helplessly with nowhere else to go.

I watched in silence as they approached. Where were my men? Where was my team? Who had my back?

But I could see I was on my own. There was no one to help me. They had deserted me long ago.

"Sam! Which method would you use?" The teacher's voice broke through my thoughts.

Suddenly alert once more, I looked at her vaguely. I knew she had said my name, but I had no idea what else she had just said. She stood at the front of the room frowning at me. While at the same time, I was sure Jake would be smirking with amusement.

"Ah, I'm sorry. What did you say?" I asked, my face turning a bright shade of red.

She shook her head with annoyance as she spoke. "Sam, please pay attention in class!"

She then turned to someone else to answer her question and I sighed with relief.

Meanwhile, Jake continued to stare. I could feel his menacing scowl burning into my skin and working its way through my senses.

Tess...

When the bell for morning recess finally sounded I remained in my seat and told Lacey that I'd catch up to her and the others shortly. She frowned curiously but didn't push the matter, then followed the other girls to the door.

That morning Miss Hodgkins had taught our class, while her class was involved in a specialist science lesson. The classes were rotating that day, and as our usual teacher, Miss Browne was absent, Miss Hodgkins had stepped in to replace her.

I knew that it was the perfect opportunity to take advantage of. Miss Hodgkins was renowned for being very strict and a lot of kids didn't like her. But after seeing her in action with kids who had done the wrong thing, I decided she was the perfect teacher to talk to. And I was sure that she would follow up on what I had to say.

Already that morning, she had raised her voice at Jake, who rarely concentrated in class and often distracted the people around him. They all thought he was funny and he was constantly trying to get a reaction. While Miss Browne tended to ignore him and was nice to everyone, Miss Hodgkins was quite the opposite.

Glancing out the classroom window while I waited for everyone to leave the room, I tried to frame the words in my head. Miss Hodgkins needed to be told about Jake's relentless bullying. But the problem went far deeper than that, and I had to make her understand how serious the situation was.

At the same time, had to ensure she realized that if something wasn't done quickly, the consequences would go beyond her control. I just didn't know how to do that without giving away Sam's secret. That had to be kept hidden at all costs. But if something wasn't done quickly, I felt quite certain the whole school would find out what he was capable of.

I thought for a moment about all the class discussions we'd had about bullying, where we were told to ignore it and walk away. That was the first step in dealing with the problem. But if it continued, we were advised to report the incident so that something could be done. This often didn't happen though, and bullying incidents went by unnoticed all the time.

Even though I wasn't the victim, I'd had enough. Ignoring and walking away hadn't worked. Trying to put Jake in his place hadn't worked either. Now I was at the report stage. It was what I knew I must do. I could not stand by and watch it go on any longer.

Standing up from my seat, I made my way towards the teacher's desk.

"Miss Hodgkins, can I please talk to you about something?"

"Yes, of course, Tess," she smiled at me. "What's the problem?"

She waited curiously for me to begin. But just as I opened my mouth to speak, I was distracted by movement outside the room.

The wind was howling furiously. While at the same time groups of kids were huddled together against buildings and in various nooks and crannies, in an attempt to shelter from the weather. For a brief moment, I registered how cold and miserable it looked out there.

But what had caught my eye was the sight of Jake Collins, who was standing within a few feet of Sam. They looked like a pair of angry beasts, ready to attack, each one waiting for the other to make a move.

From my spot alongside Miss Hodgkins' desk, I had a clear view of the area. And I could see the trees blowing at right-angles in the wind. As if picking up on the same thoughts as me, Sam looked upwards and stared for a second at the overhanging branches just a few feet away.

As if in sync with what was going on in his head, or perhaps somehow he had transferred his thoughts to my own, I focused on the massive tree branches that seemed to bend and sway above him.

I stared with dread at the sight before me. I had seen tree branches fall around Jake before. Surely this was not going to happen again.

But instead of a tree branch, it seemed that the metal sheeting from a nearby overhead awning had come loose, and as if in slow motion, I watched it tear from its hinges and fly through the air, as easily as if it were a small twig on a breezy day.

The large sheet of metal was not a tiny twig though. It was a heavy and dangerous missile and it was heading in Jake's direction. I stared in horror as the scene unfolded, while at the same time, Jake glared at Sam, completely unaware of the danger heading towards him.

***

**Find out what happens next in
The Secret - Book 4
Available SOON!**

*Thank you so much for reading this book. I hope that you really enjoyed it. If you did, would you mind leaving a review. I'd really appreciate it!
Thanks so much!
Katrina x*

Like us on Facebook…
Julia Jones Diary
Free Books For Kids

And follow us on Instagram
**@juliajonesdiary
@freebooksforkids**

Here are some more great books that I hope you enjoy.

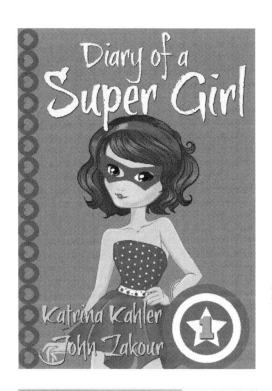

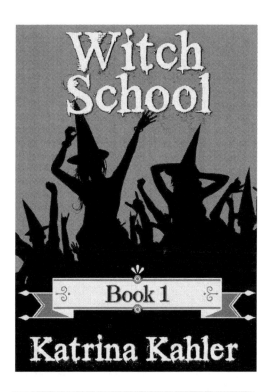

13007084R00164

Printed in Great Britain
by Amazon